I0822671

THE BLACK CASKET

GIORGIO BORLENGHI

FEDERICA BORLENGHI

"It is charming to disembark at the polished steps of a little campo – a sunny, shabby square with an old well in the middle, an old church on one side and tall Venetian windows looking down"

— HENRY JAMES

ACKNOWLEDGMENTS

There are so many I would like to thank for helping me tell this story better, ...and frankly tell it at all.

Federica, you took a passionate idea and orchestrated wonderful characters all around it.
Carolyn, you made it go from just words to reality.
Mike, your literary advice was invaluable, you left us too soon my friend.
Cathy, you came with me to Venice way too many times, and patiently allowed me to express my love for this one-of-a-kind city.

And you Venice thanks for loving me back, with every calle, every bridge, every campo, every building, every church, each and every rainy day.

CONTENTS

CHAPTER ONE

VENICE – MAY 5TH 1432

In the huge expanse of Saint Mark's Square, Venice, a crowd was gathering—a crowd that wanted far more than its daily supply of brown trout or fleshy sturgeon.

A crescendo was slowly building, a gaggle of cat calls and braying chants, coupled with raucous jeers and grunts of sneering contempt. The air above the bobbing heads was filled with raised fists thrust skyward, knuckles white beneath calloused thumbs. Wives and mothers waved Venetian flags depicting the golden lion of Saint Mark holding a long sword, set against a red backdrop with six woven gold fringes representing the six regions of the city.

The sound of drums filled the air, a slow, repetitive rhythm that stirred the crowd into even greater voice.

Somewhere, a woman yelled, "Traitor!" and a gruff man called out, '"For Venice!"

The crowd jostled in front of the Palazzo Ducale, which dominated the vista with its sweeping arches, open first-floor loggias, and herring bone-pattern paving. It was the home of the doge, the highest official of the Republic of Venice, and the most revered building in the city. Beside it, jutting out from among the roaring spectators, were two giant columns standing over forty feet tall. Atop the right-hand gray granite column was the bronze depiction of the Lion of Saint Mark, and atop the left-hand monolith was a statue carved from pink stone of Saint Theodore Tiron, the patron saint of the city. The saint was holding a spear and standing on top of a recently defeated dragon. Beneath him, the crowd roared as the executioner dressed in black emerged from the palace.

The sea of people parted as the cloaked and hooded man carried a heavy axe in both hands, walking slowly and with purpose, glancing only occasionally at those who lined his path. His heavy boots scraped against the stone paving, and the hem of his cloak created a black wake that followed like the premonition of death behind him. He didn't pause, and he didn't speak. His silence was punctuated only by the squawk of the gulls soaring overhead.

With his journey completed, he climbed the steps to the raised platform that housed the execution block and rested his axe against his hip, hands folded in front of him. With the crowd now more thirsty for blood than ever, he turned his head to the palace and offered a curt nod.

The giant palace doors flew open, pushed aside by six armored guards wearing the colors of the Venetian army, heavy swords strapped to their belts by ornate scabbards and red and gold shields held by their sides. They gripped their spears perpendicular to their bodies to drive away the crowd that clamored to get the first glance of the prisoner, the man whose life would be ended before the night was over. More guards emerged, and two by two, they formed a pathway leading from the palace doors to the executioner's platform. They pushed the crowd back, using their weapons as blockades as the angry faces grew more animated and the jeers from the back began to grow in intensity.

When the prisoner emerged from the darkness of the doorway, those jeers became hate-filled curses and raging cries of blood and torment. Ordinarily God-fearing people turned into ravenous, bloodthirsty monsters, waving clawed hands and pounding fists while uttering coarse obscenities decrying the moral integrity of the man dressed in a dark tunic and velvet beret, his hands manacled by heavy irons behind him.

"Kill him!" somebody cried.

"Throw his body into the lagoon!" another yelled.

"The executioner's blade is too good for him!"

Meanwhile, the drummers continued their slow crescendo, steady beats five seconds apart that punctuated the roars and deafening cries.

Two guards stood on either side of the prisoner, their hands placed beneath his arms. The prisoner's mouth was blocked by a mordacchia—a thick wooden stick placed between his teeth and strapped to his skull by coarse leather. Blood dripped from the prisoner's lips, which were swollen and split. His eyes scanned the animated spectators but remained defiant. He stood motionless except for the gradual rise and fall of his chest. The crowd was at full volume now, a roar so deafening it seemed to reach to the heavens. The drummers continued their heavy pounding but quickened their pace, the rapid tempo resembling the hooves of a dozen horses stampeding from the north.

"Traitor!" the lead guard hollered, inciting the crowd further.

"The Count of Carmagnola deserves to die!" a man shouted in response.

The guards moved, half-dragging the prisoner as they hurried. The count tried to keep up, but the strength in his legs seemed to falter, and he stumbled.

"Come on!" the guard yelled, rebuking him. "Unless, of course, you want to show the whole of Venice how pathetic you are!"

The count responded by righting himself, thrusting his chin forward, and puffing out his chest. He turned to the crowd and nodded, eyes steely and determined. These had once been his people. This had been his city. He loved the narrow alleyways, the busy canals, the bustling squares and busy markets. The citizens here had shown him such love and good faith after everything that had happened to him and his wife. How had it all come to this?

They walked on, passing the first column, following the path marked out for them. Suddenly, the executioner's platform came into view. His stomach turned as he saw the axe, the dull blade resting beside the block where his head would soon be placed.

He peered all around him. The people looked like strangers to him, men and women he could never hope to know. Their eyes were hungry, their mouths snarling and spiteful. Somebody spat at him. Spittle dappled his face and chest. The crowd roared its approval, and a hate-fueled woman screamed at him, "Traditore!"

Then *she* was there. His wife. Antonia. He could see her through the throng, her eyes filled with tears, her lips trembling. She wore her red robes over a silk under-gown. His heart broke at the sight of her. His love, the woman he adored more than life itself. He wanted to go to her, to take her in his arms and tell her everything would be okay, but how could he? How could he escape from the soldiers' clutches and flee this baying mob? They had gone through so much together, he and his Antonia, so many troubles, and yet every time, they had found a way to make something good from the destruction they had left behind. This time was different, however. There was no escape route. There were no horses to carry them to safety; there was no duke or nobleman offering them protection in exchange for his services; there was no palace to hide inside or a city where they could disappear like shadows. There was a grim finality to this situation, a gut-wrenching certainty.

"My husband!" Antonia cried. "He is my husband! I beg you, let me embrace him!"

The count pulled his chains and tried in vain to go to her, but the soldier hauled him back, striking him across the shoulders with a cudgel.

"Stay where you are, prisoner!" he yelled. "Guards, see that this woman does not interfere with the execution."

Two soldiers pushed his wife back as he was led to the steps. Above him, the executioner peered down at him from beneath the shadowy confines of his black hood. The count had seen this play out many times before, but he had never foreseen that one day he too would be climbing these steps to certain death.

"Bring him to me," the executioner said. "Drive him to his knees."

The count looked up and saw his wife screaming his name, her face stricken with despair, and then he felt the heavy blow to the backs of his legs, and he dropped to the ground. A hand on the back of his head pushed him forward, and he felt the cold kiss of the elm wood, the indentation that had been made by the axe's heavy head as it had sliced through the necks of its prior victims.

Terror gripped him with the the icy fingers of the reaper's gloved hand. He was moments away from walking through the gates to heaven's kingdom, and although that thought filled him with a glorious hope, it did not assuage the fear that enveloped his still-beating heart. He could hear Antonia's voice, but it was buried beneath a tumultuous crescendo of jeers and cruel chants. The crowd would not be silenced until his head was removed from his neck. The idea brought sour bile to his throat, but he wouldn't give the bloodthirsty audience the satisfaction of seeing the fear leaving his body in a stream of vomit.

From the balcony of the great palace, the doge appeared, causing a huge cheer of approval from the crowd. He held out his hands to silence them and looked down at the count, his gaze steadfast and emotionless.

"You know why you are here," he said. "And you know the crimes for which you are being punished. Your treacherous behavior deserves no other fate than that which faces you." He raised his arm as a darkness passed over his features. "May your heart be purified by the executioner's blade."

As his hand came down, the axe swished through the air, and the count bit down on the mordacchia and said a silent prayer for the wife and daughters he would never see again.

Antonia cried out in anguish as the blade cut through her husband's neck but did not break all the way through. His head lopped to one side, unseeing eyes gazing at her as blood pumped from the severed artery. Muscle, sinew, and what remained of his spinal cord kept his head from falling from the block. His body jerked and spasmed like a bucking horse.

"Leave him!" she screamed. "In the name of God, leave him be!"

She gripped her daughters' hands, Luchina and Antonietta, turning their heads away from the gruesome sight. Tears fell from Luchina's eyes, and Antonietta sobbed in silence, her shoulders shuddering at the violent grief that rippled through her body.

Above them, the executioner raised the axe again and this time brought it down with even more force. The crowd erupted with a rapturous roar, but still the blade did not cut all the way through. Antonia almost collapsed from the trauma, but one of the solders held her upright. Luchina screamed, and Antonietta cried out. Antonia hugged them to her bosom to prevent them from seeing their father's plight. Her husband's head was now hanging by a single sliver of bloodied flesh and crushed vertebrae, but still it did not tumble. She could feel every blow, sense every agonizing cut.

Somebody in front of her lost control of his stomach, and a woman standing beside her collapsed. A man cried out as more blood spurted from the wounded neck while another man laughed, pointing at her husband's head as it swung side to side, dangling on the remaining muscle and bone.

"Come," she said to the girls, knowing there was nothing more she could do for her beloved. "We need to leave."

The crowd were too distracted by the senseless violence to notice her pushing through them and dragging her two young girls with her. They had to get away. If she remained in the square after everything was done, there was no telling what these crazed Venetians might do to her. The girls were her priority now. She couldn't let anything happen to them.

Just as they neared the rear of the Piazza, she heard the executioner roar once more, and she turned to see the final blow. This time, the blade went all the way through and embedded itself in the hard wood. As the crowd screamed and cried out, her husband's head tumbled and spun, falling through the air in a hail of blood and splintered bone. Antonia's whole world fell away from her. As the head rolled into the wicker basket, she stifled her sobs, gripped her girls' hands, and ran, as fast as her trembling legs would carry her.

CHAPTER TWO

MILAN – PRESENT DAY

"Sister, you make me laugh more than anyone I know!" Mauro Imperi cried in his native Italian tongue, slapping the table hard as tears streamed down his cheeks. "How I've missed your sense of humor."

"It's you who are telling the jokes," his sister, Federica replied, her own laughter kissing her dark eyes and the corners of her grinning mouth. She turned to her daughter, Costanza, who was looking at her mother and uncle, her face aghast. "And the moral of that story is you should never ask your Uncle Mauro for medical advice."

"Oh, don't worry," Costanza replied, sweeping her long dark hair to one side. "I don't intend to."

"Don't be so hard on me, Costanza," Mauro said, still laughing. "One day you may find my wisdom useful."

"When that day comes, I'll be sure to let you know," Costanza said, pushing her chair back as she collected the empty dishes from the table.

Mauro eyed his younger sister. He hadn't seen her for such a long time. These days, he rarely made it to Milan. His home in Houston, Texas had become such a stronghold for him, and although the city of Venice was a familiar haunt—one that he'd frequented more and more in recent times—the trip west to Milan from the ancient city was one he rarely troubled himself with. It wasn't that he didn't miss Federica and her daughter; it was just that he'd been so preoccupied lately.

"You know, I really should come here more often. I'm sorry that I haven't."

"Don't worry about it," Federica said, flapping a hand dismissively. "It's not like we ever fly to Houston to see you."

"True, but you're my family, and this was my home once, too."

"I'm sure Milan misses you as much as you miss it."

Mauro nodded. He'd had some happy times here. Some troubled ones, too.

"This dinner was so beautiful," he said. "The pasta, the tomato sauce. I miss your table more than I miss Milan."

Federica laughed once more, touching her brother's hand, her eyes taking him in.

"Why do you think I'm marrying Costanza?" a woman with shoulder-length auburn hair and a strong British accent replied.

"You're marrying me, Mia, because you love me," Costanza said, resting her hands on her fiancée's slim shoulders.

"That and your famous risotto," Mia joked, smiling. "Honestly, they don't make Italian food in England like they do in Milan."

"And neither should they," Mauro said. "Fish and chips will never compete with our Risotto alla Milanese."

"True," Costanza said. "But, honestly, eating a crispy piece of cod doused in salt and vinegar while sitting on the beach does come a pretty close second."

Mauro smiled, watching as his niece and her partner gave each other the kind of looks he'd once shared with his wife, Susan. He missed those times. He missed the tender touches, the endless conversation, and the soft kisses beneath the stars.

Mia tried to kick back from her own chair and grab the empty bowl of salad, but Costanza stayed her hand.

"Hey," she said. "You don't get to clean up. You're a guest."

"And as a guest, I want to help," Mia replied.

"Then keep my uncle talking," Costanza said and laughed. "The more occupied he is, the less trouble he can get into."

"That's not fair," Mauro said, tossing his napkin on the table. "I can get into some pretty deep shit even if I am preoccupied."

"True," Federica chimed in. "I've seen this guy get arrested while still debating the pros and cons of a ruling monarchy with his college roommates."

"What did you get arrested for?" Mia asked, seemingly shocked at the revelation.

"That was a long time ago, sister, and you know it," Mauro said, before turning to Mia. "And to answer your question, sometimes the warm embrace of a good glass of Chianti can get the better of my good judgement."

"Your niece knows all about that, right, Cos?" Mia laughed.

As the frivolity died down and the table was cleared, Federica turned to her brother. "You still haven't told me while you're here. Has something happened?"

"What, I can't come and see my sister without there being some sort of problem?" Mauro replied.

"No, of course not. It's just that you didn't even give me time to get your room ready."

"It's no problem. I'll sleep on the couch if I have to. I don't want you to go to any trouble."

"Nonsense. It's no trouble at all. It's just that when you turn up out of the blue like this, it makes me think that there might be something you're not telling me."

Mauro took his sister's hand in his. "Trust me, Federica, if there was a story to tell, you would be the first person I'd tell it to."

Federica's eyes narrowed. "Why, then? There has to be a reason."

"Okay, then," Mauro said, nodding slowly. "If you must know, I'm heading back to the old city in the morning."

"To Venice?"

"That's right."

"Again?"

"What can I say? It seems that even when I'm over 5,000 miles away, that old town keeps calling my name."

"I love Venice," Mia replied. "I went there with some university pals a couple of years go. Such history, such architecture."

"And that's not even the half of it," Mauro replied, delighted by the young woman's enthusiasm.

"Why are you going to Venice?" Federica asked.

"Must I have a reason?"

"An explanation, at least."

Mauro folded his arms and leaned back in his chair. "Maybe I just want to wander."

"Nonsense," Federica said. "You've wandered those streets more times than I can count. You don't fly 5,000 miles to wander when you can do that on your own doorstep."

"I don't get it," Mia said. "What's wrong with Venice?"

"Precisely," Mauro replied. "What's wrong with Venice, dear sister?"

"Nothing's wrong with it, of course," Federica said. "But it's like my brother can't stay away. And what about family time?"

"Isn't this family time?" Mauro asked. "This dinner? This conversation? How much family time do you want?"

"More than just a few hours," Federica said. "More than just a chat over a dinner table. You said it yourself—we haven't seen you for such a long time, and yet you choose to leave us to go to a place you've frequented more than your own hometown."

Mauro played with the wine cork, turning it back and forth like a compass. "You're starting to sound like my wife."

Federica's head jerked sharply to her daughter as she sipped her wine. Costanza stood in the archway between the dining room and kitchen, dishcloth gripped in her clenched hands. After a few moments, she rolled her eyes and went back to her chores.

"I'd love to see it again," Mia said. "Venice, I mean. I hardly got to spend any time there during our tour of northern Italy."

"Tell me, Mia, do you travel much?" Mauro asked.

"Not as much as I'd like to," she replied. "But that's something Cos and I are hoping to do once I get a job that pays the kind of money that will cover it."

"Well, Venice is the kind of city you need to take in slowly," Mauro replied. "The history there, it can't be rushed."

"Maybe you should go with Mauro," Federica blurted out. "Tomorrow. It's only a short ride on the train from here. A little over three hours. You could be there before lunchtime if you leave early."

"Really?" Mia asked, her head swiveling from Federica to Mauro. "You would take me with you?"

Mauro looked taken aback. "Well, I don't know about that. I couldn't possibly—"

"Sure you could," Federica replied. "You could give Mia the guided tour, what with you being such a regular visitor. You must show her what she missed the last time. Mauro knows the city so well, Mia. His wife is a very well-known art historian and collector. She curated part of a Biennale a while ago. And did you know, Mauro, that Mia here graduated in Art History at the Accademia di Brera?"

"I did not know that," Mauro replied, now more interested in their British guest. "Congratulations, Mia. That is indeed a fine accomplishment."

"Oh, she is brilliant!" Federica said without waiting for Mia to respond. "She's a fantastic researcher, and as she says, she has been desperately looking for a job. Maybe you have some friends to connect her to in Venice, Mauro. Are you still in touch with Susan's friends? The ones from the Biennale? Or maybe you still have contacts from the auctions you used to go to? It would be so great. How long are you staying there?"

Mauro had the feeling he was being played, but he also had to admit that having a beautiful and well-qualified researcher traveling with him was hardly an inconvenience. Mia could be the perfect foil for what he had in mind.

"Well, I do have a confession to make," he said. "I actually haven't purchased my return ticket yet."

"Splendid!" Federica exclaimed. "That's even better news." She turned to Mia. "Just go, my dear. I might even join you myself on the weekend. I haven't been in such a long time."

The suggestion that his sister might accompany him along with Costanza's fiancée prompted Mauro into action. "Well if it's going to be such a big gathering, why don't you invite the whole family?"

The sarcasm wasn't lost on his sister. "Well, if the mountain doesn't go to Maometto..."

"I'm sorry," Mia said, looking confused. "I don't understand the reference."

"Never mind that," Federica said. "Will you go?"

Mia looked at each of them in turn, her lips pursed together, one eyebrow raised. "I mean, it would be kinda fun, but I wouldn't want to intrude on Signore Imperi's trip."

"Nonsense!" Federica interjected, cutting her brother off from responding. "I'm getting your tickets. Mauro, what time are you planning on leaving?"

"As early as the trains will allow," Mauro replied, suddenly wanting to get away from his sister as soon as possible.

Costanza arrived back from the kitchen, smiling as her eyes scanned the exchange. "Coffee, anyone?" she asked, before realizing she'd been left out of an important discussion. "Okay, so what did I miss?"

"Are you busy tomorrow?" her mother asked.

"Busy? Why? Is something happening?"

"Just answer the question, dear."

"I guess I'll be writing my thesis, just like every other day."

"Then maybe it's time to take a break."

Costanza turned to Mia, her brow furrowed. "Mia, can you fill me in here?"

Mia took her partner's hand, her broad smile stretching from ear to ear. "Oh, Costanza," she replied. "Didn't you hear? We're going to Venice."

Mauro studied his journal as the bullet train sped along the tracks, the countryside flying past in a blur of green and brown. The trio had managed to get seats close together. While Mia and Costanza sipped their tepid coffee, Mauro had his head stuck in his book. He had a lot of important things to consider, not least how he would go ahead with his plan while accommodating his newly appointed traveling companions.

"Thank you so much for allowing us to come with you," Mia said, placing her cup on the table between them. "I'm really excited about seeing Venice again."

"I agree," Costanza added. "Mia and I have been looking for a place to spend some time together, and what better place than La Serenissima, right?"

Mauro looked up from his book and reached into his pocket for his handkerchief. He dabbed at his brow, which was moist with sweat. There was so much to consider, so much to think about, and yet here these two women were, talking about how they could make this trip into some sort of romantic getaway.

"The pleasure is all mine," he said before returning to his research. He had so many notes to read through, so much detail, so much history. His wife had helped him pull it all together, but he needed to assemble it in his head in a way that made sense and could be useful to him.

"Costanza told me how there's been no update about your wife," Mia said. "I am so truly sorry about what happened to her."

Mauro didn't look up from his book, although he could sense Costanza glaring at her fiancée.

"No, nothing so far," he replied, attempting to deflect the conversation.

"Hopefully they'll find her soon," Mia pressed.

"At this rate, I'll be an old man before she comes home."

"Uncle!" Costanza exclaimed.

"What? It's true."

"I can tell you that Mom almost collapsed when she found out Susan was missing," Costanza said, the sorrow evident in her eyes.

"That's why I never told her about my hospitalization," Mauro said, realizing too late that he'd said too much.

"Hospitalization?"

He held out his hands and tried to pacify his niece. "Don't worry, it was nothing serious."

"Hold on. Wind back," Costanza said. "You've been unwell?"

"A heart attack, but only a little one. You know how these doctors like to exaggerate, especially when money's involved."

"When did it happen?" Mia asked.

"A few days ago. Last weekend, actually."

"Last weekend?" Costanza cried. "You mean, you had a heart attack less than a week ago, and yet you thought it was a good idea to get on a plane and fly to Italy?"

"My doctor said it should be okay."

"Should be or will be?"

"Costanza, I really think you're overreacting. At my age, these things happen."

Mia reached out and took his hand in hers. "How long were you in the hospital?"

Mauro huffed. "Three days, no more, and here I am, not five days later, and in the peak of health. They were talking about bypass surgery, but what do they know? I'm as fit as I was when I was a sixteen-year-old boy."

There was a clatter and a rattle as a server pushed a trolley up the aisle. The cart was laden with alcoholic drinks, hot coffee, and sweet-smelling food.

"A drink, madams? Sir?"

"I'll have an espresso," Mauro replied, reaching into his pocket for his wallet.

"Do you really think you should be having that?" Costanza said, looking up at the server with concern etched into her face. "My zio hasn't been very well."

"Don't listen to her," Mauro replied, handing over his money. "She's a little crazy."

The server poured the hot drink in silence, and as she trundled away, Mauro sipped his coffee and glared at the two women.

"Under no circumstances must you breathe a word of this to my sister, you understand?"

"The heart attack or the coffee?" Costanza asked, stubbornly folding her arms.

"Either," Mauro replied. "Now, if you don't mind, I have some reading to do."

As the train headed toward its ultimate destination, Mauro buried his head in his book and hoped that, pretty soon, he would see the culmination of all his efforts. It had been so long, after all.

CHAPTER THREE
VENICE – 1432

The crowd had dispersed into the night. The creeping darkness had the piazza in its icy grip. A breeze swept a cluster of litter and leaves from the floor and cast it to the stone walls. Overhead, the penny moon shone brightly, a sliver of cloud passing over it like smoke. Beneath the stars, the bloodied stage stood still and silent, a timber visage soaked in tragedy and violence. The body was slumped over the block. The basket beneath it was filled with skull, flesh, and gore-soaked hair. Overhead, the gulls cawed and swooped, casting wide, soaring shadows over the morbid scene beneath them.

Two men approached from the north, one holding a linen sheet, another a large hessian sack. They were pushing a two-wheeled cart in front of them. The men were dressed in guard uniforms but were unarmed. They stopped before the stage and lowered their eyes, tipping their hats before climbing the steps. The old wooden stairs creaked beneath their heavy boots. A rat scurried from beneath them, shooting the two men an anxious glance before heading toward the water.

"Damn vermin will be running this city before the year's out," the first guard, Jacopo, said.

They looked down at the decapitated body, at the fine clothes stained crimson, the polished leather boots, and the severed head that peered up at them from within the mop of auburn hair. The count's eyes were wide open, accusing them with a glare that screamed betrayal.

"What's he looking at?" the second guard, Matteo, asked, flinching as he stared at the count's face.

"Got what was coming to him, if you ask me," Jacopo replied.

They collected the basket, tipped the head into the sack, and then covered the body with the linen sheet. Once the corpse was fully embraced by the makeshift shroud, they stooped down, collected the package, and slipped it into the thick sack. With everything ready, they carried the fully-covered cadaver to the cart and placed it inside.

"To the canal," Jacopo said. "The boat will be waiting."

At the landing, close to the Bridge of Sighs, they awaited the vessel's arrival. Jacopo was anxious. They had been told to get the count out of the city as quickly as possible so as not to attract the attention of those that might sympathize with the count's treacherous ways, but the whole exercise was taking way too long. If the boat didn't arrive before sunrise, they would be forced to take the corpse back to the palace and confess they had failed in their task. The doge was not a man to be crossed, and unfortunately for them, he had a long memory.

"Here it is," Matteo said. "I can see it moving through the shadows."

They pushed the cart toward the canal's edge and waited patiently, watching as the boat glided through the calm water as silently as a cat stalking its prey.

"Finally," Jacopo said to the boat's single occupant. "We thought you'd gotten lost."

The two men hauled the body from the cart and, with the help of the third man, lowered it into the vessel. The boat rocked from side to side as the body rolled onto the floor, coming to a stop by the captain's feet.

"Inside," Jacopo said to his companion. "I'd like to get this finished before my wife realizes I'm not there for breakfast."

"Wait!" a man cried from the darkness. The guards whirled to the sound, and as the clatter of footsteps grew louder, a man in the brown, hooded garb of a religious order appeared.

"Fra Dolphi," Jacopo said. "What brings you to the bridge at this late hour?"

"You have the count in your boat, do you not?" the friar asked.

The guards glanced anxiously at each other. "Yes. I will confess, the traitor's body is in the sack."

"Where are you taking him?"

Matteo leaned over and spat onto the ground. "Where he belongs."

"No, no. That isn't right," the friar replied. "I won't allow that."

Jacopo stepped from the boat. "We have our orders, friar, and we plan to follow them to the letter."

"And I have a request from the family to inter the body at my church."

"And why would they ask that of you?" Matteo asked disdainfully.

"Because I am the family's confessor."

The guards glanced at each other once more, unsure what to do. If this man was the family's confessor, then surely he had the right to say where the body was buried, but it was also unusual for the clergy to get involved in the internment of a traitor. Finally, Jacopo asked, "You want us to take this man to the Basilica of Santa Maria Gloriosa dei Frari?"

The friar nodded his agreement. "As I said, it is the family's wish."

"You will lead us there?" Jacopo asked.

"Are we really going to do what this guy asks?" Matteo hissed, shooting the friar an angry glance.

Jacopo shrugged nonchalantly. "The guy's dead. Why should anyone care where he's buried?"

"The doge will care."

"The doge won't know, and the quicker we get this done, the happier everyone will be."

Matteo shook his head but offered nothing by way of argument.

"Very well, then," the friar said, stepping onto the boat and taking a seat beside the body. "Let's make haste."

It took them less than half an hour to make it to the basilica, with the night still heavy overhead. The church stood before them, a tall tower beside a sweeping pinnacle, topped by three white summits that stretched toward the heavens. A large circular window surrounded by three smaller openings looked out across the dark water like the eyes of a silent watcher. At the side of the canal, a group of young friars stood, their heads hooded and bowed. Jacopo turned to Matteo and frowned.

"It seems these people have been preparing for this ever since the execution was announced," he said to Matteo. "I say we go along with whatever they want and get away from here as soon as we can."

"And if anyone asks?" Matteo replied.

"Then we say nothing. This secret dies with us, okay?"

As the boat drew against the dock and the men tied it to the cleats, the young friars stepped onto the vessel, collected the body in the sack, and hastily carried it toward the church.

"Okay, my good fellows," the friar said, stepping from the boat and raising his hood. "At this point, there's nothing left to say, other than to wish you both a good night."

He walked away, leaving the guards to watch the young friars in the distance as they approached a door in the side of the church, glancing up and down the street before disappearing inside, leaving merely a memory of their involvement.

"Let's go home," Jacopo said to the captain. "The quicker we forget this ever happened, the better it will be for all of us."

Once inside, the friars moved to the first cloister and gradually lowered the sack containing the body to the ground while waiting for Fra Dolphi to arrive. They stood around the corpse, their heads lowered, while the darkness of the church's shadow enveloped them.

"Good work," Fra Dolphi whispered as he appeared beside them. "Now we must carry out the family's wishes."

On the ground, there was a wide area marked out by small stones. The friars disappeared for a few moments, and when they returned, they carried a large maple casket. They placed it on the ground, lowered the body into it, and sealed the lid. Once done, they dug a deep hole where the earth had been marked, pausing only to catch their breaths before continuing on, digging deeper and deeper until they had excavated at least six feet of earth.

The first friar pulled two straps from his gown and pushed one end of each beneath the casket, gesturing for the friars opposite to take the strain. Then they hoisted the casket aloft, walked it to the deep grave, and lowered it inside, allowing it to nestle gently on the dry earth.

Fra Dolphi approached, drew the sign of the cross over his chest, and signaled for the others to lower their heads.

"We commit this man's earthly body into your loving hands. Grant him eternal rest in Your Kingdom where no pain or sorrow exists. May the light of Your face shine upon him, and may he find peace in Your presence. Comfort his family who mourn, reminding us that death is but a passage to eternal life. We ask this through Christ our Lord, who conquered death. Amen."

The friars repeated the final affirmation, then shoveled earth onto the coffin, raking leaves and branches on top of the mound so that its presence was hidden. As they departed, Fra Dolphi looked down at the count's resting place and nodded somberly. They had done what was asked of them. Surely that was all they could do.

Little did he know that the night's endeavors were just the beginning of a long and arduous journey, one that would be passed from friar to friar, involve many people, and last several hundred years.

CHAPTER FOUR

VENICE – PRESENT DAY

The vaporetto raced across the water, its belly filled with dozens of visitors wanting to see Palazzo Ducale, San Marco Basilica, and the infamous Bridge of Sighs. Mauro sat among them, flinching as the thickset American tourist next to him tried to reach for something in his bag, pushing him into the English tourist on the other side, who was trying to take a photograph.

"Dio mio!" he exclaimed. "I'll be happy when I set foot on dry land."

The boat headed across the waterway, passing a group of gondolas at the head of a canal, the gondoliers dressed in striped shirts, black hats, and dark pants. Beside them, a group of diners clinked their glasses of Aperol Spritz and cheered before tucking into platefuls of delicious pasta and sumptuous pizza. Atop one of the bridges, a young couple paused to take a selfie photograph, the young woman holding her phone on a stick raised high above them to get the best view of the beautiful scenery. On the other side of the waterway, a human statue spraypainted silver posed for the onlookers, only to surprise a child who tried to touch him by bowing his head and holding out his hand. An older couple walked along the edge of the water, eating from tall cones of strawberry gelato and idly chatting. Before them sat a wide building with open balconies and shuttered windows. The sign above the door read Hotel Danieli.

"That's it!" Mia exclaimed. "That's where we're staying. Oh, Costanza, look how beautiful it is."

"It really is something," Costanza replied. "You really came through for us, Zio."

"Only the best for my niece and her fiancée," Mauro said, pushing his journal back into his case before hauling himself from his seat, happy to be away from the big American and the nosy Englishwoman. "Now, I hope you brought your walking shoes."

Costanza eyed her uncle. "Why would you say that?"

Mauro smiled. "Because you'll be needing them."

Mia slung her case on the large double bed and opened it, pulling dresses, trousers, tops, and other assorted clothes from its belly and hanging them excitedly on hangers that she hooked onto the closet rail. She could barely believe the opulence of the hotel. It was like something from a Hollywood movie, a building steeped in rich Venetian history, but it also had an air of class and sophistication. The mini-bar was well-stocked, the coffee machine served the best espressos, and the bed looked as soft as the finest cotton.

"Darling, do you want me to put your things away also?" she asked, glancing at Costanza, who was standing on the balcony, anxiously smoking a cigarette. A seagull swooped toward her, causing Costanza to blow smoke, flapping a hand to chase the irritating bird away. She scrolled through her phone, seemingly agitated by what she was reading.

"Is something wrong?" Mia asked.

"It's just my mother," Costanza said. "Asking for photographs already, as if we've actually had a chance to take any."

"I'm sure she's just trying to take an interest," Mia said. "You said yourself, she hasn't been to Venice in such a long time."

Costanza set her phone on the coffee table and crushed out her cigarette, thin wisps of smoke wafting into the air like strands of silk. "It's not that."

"Then what is it, love?" Mia asked, wrapping her arms around her partner's slim waist.

"He had a heart attack, Mia. My Zio. Why would he keep something like that a secret from his family?"

"I guess because he didn't want you to worry," Mia replied. "He was thinking of you both."

"He was being selfish. He should have realized we would want to know something as important as that."

"So you could fuss over him?"

"So we could stop him doing something stupid. Like flying from America to Italy."

"And if he hadn't, we wouldn't be here," Mia replied, pulling Costanza close with one arm and gesturing toward the entrancing cityscape with the other. "I mean, just look at it. It's beautiful."

"Precisely," Costanza replied. "Beauty isn't what Zio Mauro needs. He should be in a hospital, or at the very least, at home with his son, convalescing."

Mia exhaled loudly and plucked the phone from the table. She held it up, made sure the city was visible behind them, and smiled, snapping a picture as she did so.

"Mia!"

She interrupted Costanza's objection by kissing her tenderly, running her hands through her hair as the late afternoon breeze drifted across the balcony.

"Now," she whispered. "Send that photograph to your mother. Wash your face, put on something cute, and meet me downstairs. We are meeting your uncle in ten."

Costanza's expression softened, realizing her partner wasn't in the mood for a debate. "Yes, ma'am."

Mia winked at her churlishly and walked seductively toward the bedroom door. Costanza paused, feigning disinterest, before racing after her, making a grab for her as Mia skipped out of the way, laughing uncontrollably as they both tumbled onto the bed, falling and giggling, arms wrapped around each other as if they couldn't bear to be apart.

They stood outside, Costanza in a brightly colored summer dress and Mia in tight-fitting jeans and a smart top.

"You know, if I'd known Zio Mauro was going to keep us waiting, we could have—"

"Costanza!" Mia replied, smiling. "We didn't have time, and in any case, let's not forget your uncle is paying for this trip."

Before Costanza had a chance to reply, Mauro came pacing from the hotel entrance, descending the steps two at a time before heading down the Riva Degli Schiavoni without uttering a word.

"Good evening to you, too, Uncle," Costanza said.

"No time to talk," Mauro replied. "We have things to do and places to visit."

Mia dragged Costanza behind her, pausing to shoot her fiancée an amused smirk. "Where are you taking us?" she asked.

Mauro proceeded a little further before pausing and turning. His complexion was a little flushed, and beads of sweat had formed on his forehead, his hair slick to the skin. Costanza gripped Mia's hand to get her attention, her face a mask of harried concern.

"As I said," Mauro replied, dabbing his head and neck with a handkerchief. "We must hurry. Just follow me."

"But, Zio—"

"No Zio. Just move."

They proceeded along the river's edge while tourists bustled all around them, some carrying bags filled with trinkets and items of clothing, others wearing "I Love Venice" T-shirts, many with baseball caps depicting the city's most popular attractions. They weaved through the crowd as Mauro barged into anybody standing in his way. Mia thought he looked like a man on a mission and quietly wondered why Costanza's uncle was in such a rush. After all, he'd been to Venice many times before, and as far as she was aware, they didn't have an appointment to meet anybody.

"This way," Mauro said, taking them across a bridge that led to a large white building with tall arches and big windows. One side overlooked the river; the other overlooked Piazza San Marco.

"Look at this place," Mia said. "It's really something."

Despite her delight, Mauro didn't pause, racing past the historic building, ignoring the towering Campanile di San Marco, and seemingly not giving any thought to the hundreds of years of history surrounding them. Mia spied the Basilica di San Marco on their right with its large domed roof and beautifully intricate architecture, and then the square itself that was lined with numerous cafes and restaurants, each filled to the brim with hundreds of eager clientele. On the stage, a band played, the pianist leading the cellist and violinist expertly through a traditional Italian ballad.

Mauro led them down more narrow streets, crossing several canals, passing La Fenice Theatre and the Chiesa di Santo Stefano with its striking apexed roof and circular turret. They crossed the Campo Santo Stefano that was also filled with dozens of people, all eager to take photographs of yet another of Venice's star attractions, before racing toward the Gran Canal.

"Wait, Zio Mauro," Costanza cried, struggling to keep up in heels that were hardly suitable for the chase. "You're going too fast."

"We must get there before it closes," Mauro replied, barely turning to face her.

"But where?" Costanza asked. "What on Earth is so important that we must get there this evening?"

Mauro didn't answer. He merely led them to the long arch of the Accademia Bridge that overlooked the canal, where tens of tourists standing with their backs to the water, taking countless photographs that would no doubt litter the internet within seconds.

"Uncle!" Costanza yelled. "Will you just tell us where we are going?"

Mauro stopped at the center point of the bridge and turned to face them. His face was red with exertion, but his eyes were wide and alert. Mia thought he looked like a man who was about to burst with excitement.

"We are going to the most beautiful church in Venice," he said. "A place I have visited many times before, but still after all these years, it never fails to capture my imagination."

"I know where we're headed," Mia said, hand snapping instinctively into the air. "You're taking us to Santa Maria Gloriosa dei Frari, aren't you?"

Mauro's expression flickered with delight as he winked at Costanza.

"I like her," he said. "She thinks like a true Italian."

Across the water, they followed signs that led them to Scuola Di San Rocco, a gray, officious looking building with a large entranceway and tall pillars.

"This was one of the finest schools in all of Italy, with the most impressive art collection you will ever see," Mauro said. "One day, when we have time, I'll take you inside. What they have in there will blow your minds."

"Then let's take a look now," Costanza replied, looking increasingly frustrated.

"No time," Mauro said, snapping his fingers.

They followed him down a path on their right before coming upon a building that towered over them like a giant monolith. It was gothic in appearance, with three parts separated by tall pilasters, each with large round windows overlooking the canal. Above the large entranceway stood three white statues, one representing the Apostles, another a depiction of Saint Francis of Assisi, and the third of Saint Anthony of Padua.

"Here we are," Mauro declared. "The Basilica di Santa Maria Gloriosa dei Frari."

Mia stood with her hands on her hips, looking up at the impressive building. It was, indeed, the most striking church she had seen since stepping off the boat.

"Where is he going?" Costanza asked, watching as Mauro disappeared through the doorway.

"I guess we're going inside," Mia replied.

They walked through the dark archway and watched as Mauro tried to enter the basilica, ignoring the ticket booth to his right.

"Il biglietto, signore!" the attendant cried in a loud whisper. "Sir? Sir! You must pay for a ticket."

Mauro either didn't hear the man or was too entranced by what he saw to pay attention. Either way, he proceeded, oblivious to the attendant's protestations.

"Don't worry," Costanza replied, fishing around in her bag for her wallet. "He's with me. I'm paying for the three of us."

As Costanza handed over the money, Mia took in her surroundings. The basilica was too beautiful for words. She had never seen anything so stunningly gorgeous in all her life.

"Come on," Costanza said, taking her hand. "If we don't keep up, we might lose him."

They crossed over the threshold while Mia's head swiveled from side to side, trying to take in every detail, every intricately crafted sculpture, every expertly painted mural. It was like looking into a kaleidoscope and trying to pick out every color. The details were impeccable, the architecture like something from another world.

The basilica was shaped like a Roman cross and divided into three naves. Twelve large columns separated the various areas of the huge floor space with gilded arches that stretched from floor to ceiling. The high altar was decorated with a depiction of the Virgin Mary ascending to heaven, while below, the apostles watched on in awe. It was an amazing painting by Titian. A rood screen sat in front of the choir and high altar with depictions of prophets decorating its intricate marble facade. Above the rood screen, there was a sculpture of Christ on the cross, while either side of him were statues immortalizing the Virgin Mary and Saint John the Evangelist. In the right nave, there was a painting of Mary looking down on Bishop Jacopo Pesaro, while behind him, a knight was shown holding up a red flag decorated with the Papal and Pesaro coats of arms. Beside him, Saint Francis of Assisi presented the Pesaro family to Mary for her blessing.

"Pretty dark, isn't it?" Costanza said, her arms folded.

"It is, but it's kind of beautiful, too," Mia replied.

Costanza huffed. "I'm more of a red carpet girl myself."

"I don't mind a bit of glitz and glamour either, but this is history, Cos. Everything in here was created hundreds of years ago and has never been moved."

Costanza gave a curt nod of acknowledgement and then peered into the many nooks. "Have you seen my zio?"

They both scoured the segments of the basilica until Mia pointed to the right of the altar.

"There he is," she said. "He's looking at something I can't quite see."

Costanza exhaled loudly and headed off in her uncle's direction, leaving Mia trailing behind her, trying desperately to keep up. A couple studying the sculptures looked up as she passed, shaking their heads, and another tourist moved out the way as she breezed by.

Mauro was standing by a door in the right-hand aisle of the church that led to the cloister. Mia stood for a moment, watching as Costanza nudged her uncle. He seemed to ignore her and instead looked to a spot high up on the wall. Mia followed the line of his gaze and was astounded to find what looked like a black casket, dreary and unassuming, but bizarrely fixed to a spot in front of a painting of a pavilion-style canopy, its drapes pulled apart and held in place by two cherubs. Five coats of arms decorated the summit of the canopy, and in the spot where the curtains were pulled aside, a human skull was visible.

"What are we looking at?" Mia asked, taken in by this strange imagery.

"It looks like a coffin," Costanza replied, her nose turned up.

"Yes, but why here?" Mia asked. "Why fix a simple wooden coffin on a wall among these elaborate stone tombs? It's so dark and unassuming. It looks completely out of place."

"Exactly," Mauro replied. "I've always thought the same thing."

"Tell us, what exactly is it?" Mia asked.

"The thorn in my side," Mauro hissed. "The thing that occupies my mind more than anything I've ever seen before or since."

Without warning, Mauro headed back to the ticket booth, his hasty charge drawing more disapproving looks from disgruntled visitors. Once there, he tapped on the glass repeatedly.

"Hello, hello!" he bellowed impatiently. "I need to speak to the friar in charge of the Congregation of Friars."

"It's not possible," the attendant said.

"But I must insist."

"Here," the attendant replied, pushing a slip of paper through the opening. "You can send him an email if you wish."

"But this is urgent."

The attendant shrugged. "What can I tell you?"

"But this is a matter of life and death."

"Then call an ambulance," the attendant replied. "Fra Daniele does not receive visitors without an appointment."

Mauro's face turned a dark shade of red as he slammed his hand down on the counter.

"Zio!" Costanza exclaimed. "Please get a hold of yourself."

"You don't understand," Mauro said.

"Then help me to."

"Let me speak to somebody," Mauro said to the attendant, reaching for his wallet. "I have money, I can pay. Just tell me how much."

By now, a queue was forming in the doorway and the air was filled with a series of angry mutterings and groans of dissent. Mia watched as a man outside reached for his phone, and fearing the police would soon be involved, she took Mauro by the arm.

"Excuse us," she said to the people blocking their way. "Excuse us. We're leaving."

"Wait—" Mauro objected, but by now they were already outside and leaving the puzzled onlookers in their wake.

"Uncle," Costanza said when they'd managed to calm Mauro down a little. "What was all that nonsense about?"

"I'll explain," he said. "When we have time, I'll explain everything, but right now, I need to meet with the friar."

"But they told you he's not available," Costanza said. "Have you lost your mind? If you persist in being so belligerent with these people, you could find yourself in a whole world of trouble."

Costanza turned and rolled her eyes at her fiancée, but when she turned back around, Mauro was gone, racing off toward a door between the basilica and the Venetian Archives.

"What's he doing now?" Costanza asked.

Mia shrugged. "I'll give it to him," she said. "He's persistent."

Mauro reached up and rang the bell, and after a few moments, the door opened, and the face of a young friar appeared.

"Good evening," Mauro said. "I'm here to visit Fra Daniele. I have an appointment."

The young friar eyed the older man up and down and then glanced at Mia and Costanza.

"I am his cousin," Mauro lied. "I just had a heart attack, and he wanted to see me to wish me a speedy recovery."

"I... don't know," the friar said. "This is highly unusual."

"So is a heart attack," Mauro replied. "Have you had one?"

The young friar shook his head.

Mauro forced a smile. "I don't recommend it. Now... Fra Daniele?"

As the friar stood there considering his options, Mauro made the decision for him, stepping through the door as the young man watched on, shocked and confused.

More than thirty minutes passed as the pair of them stood waiting, wondering if Mauro had achieved what he had set out to do, or whether he was now in a Venetian prison waiting for somebody to come rescue him.

"He doesn't take no for an answer," Mia said, watching Costanza pace back and forth, puffing repeatedly on a cigarette.

"He's a sick man," Costanza said. "And if he keeps acting the way he is, he'll become even sicker."

"Then let's hope he gets what he wants," Mia replied, knowing that Costanza wouldn't rest until her uncle had been placated.

Suddenly the side door opened, and Mauro appeared alongside a man who Mia assumed was Fra Daniele. The young friar was beside him, his hands gripping Mauro's collar as he shoved him through the door.

"Now leave!" Fra Daniele cried. "Or I will call the police!"

Mauro stumbled into the street, his face covered in sweat and his hair unruly. He turned back to the doorway and opened his mouth to object.

"Don't you dare come back!" Fra Daniele exclaimed. "We have enough to do without having to deal with boorish Americans like you."

The door slammed, and Mauro stood there looking sheepish but defiant.

"What the hell happened in there?" Costanza yelled. "Uncle, are you okay?"

Mauro didn't answer. He just looked up at the basilica, his eyes moving back and forth as is he were running over a thousand different options in his beleaguered brain.

"Zio," Costanza said, touching her uncle's arm. "Let's get out of here. I have a bad feeling about this place."

Mauro's eyes snapped to her, and for a moment, Mia could see the old Mauro there, the man who had made them laugh over dinner and kept them entertained with his engaging stories and witty anecdotes.

"You know what?" he said. "I agree." He smoothed a hand through his hair and shot them a wide grin. "Now, the most important question is—who's hungry?"

CHAPTER FIVE

VENICE – PRESENT DAY

The restaurant was busy, every table filled with tourists, sightseers, and locals, all eager to enjoy the sumptuous delicacies that Bacaro e Trattoria da Fiore had to offer. The restaurant was renowned all over the country, and so Mauro had to pull a lot of strings to get them a table there, as well as a hefty tip he discreetly slipped the manager. The air was filled with the heady scents of grilled fish, sizzling steak, rich tomato sauce, and red wine. All around them were the sounds of animated discussions, cheerful laughter, beautiful music, and the clink-clink of cutlery and half-filled glasses. Outside, the sky was filled with a billion twinkling stars that reflected in the water like little drops of silver.

Mia looked down at her plate and marveled at the lightly battered seafood and mixed vegetables set among a light salad and slightly acidic dressing. She bit down on a succulent prawn and closed her eyes as her mouth was filled with its salty and mildly peppery taste.

"This is some place," she said. "I've heard so many good things about it, but now that I'm here, I can see that the TripAdvisor reviews hardly do it justice."

"Sergio and I go back many years," Mauro replied, slicing a strip of battered zucchini from his own plate. "Susan and I spent many beautiful evenings here, eating, drinking, and discussing the city's historic artifacts with the owner and locals."

"I'm amazed you got a table," Mia said.

Mauro winked. "Sometimes it's all about who you know."

"I was thinking about paying a visit to the Magazzini del Sale tomorrow morning," Mia said. "Would the two of you like to tag along?"

Mauro swallowed his mouthful and dabbed at his lips with a napkin. "I can't. I'm going straight back to the basilica first thing."

"What?" Costanza exclaimed, setting her cutlery down. "You can't do that. You were just thrown out of there."

"Just a little misunderstanding," Mauro replied.

"Misunderstanding? The friar told you never to come back. Zio, you have been banned from ever going there again."

He slipped another mouthful between his teeth and waved his fork at her. "It's no problem. The friars are usually not there first thing in the morning anyway."

"And what about the attendant?"

"They're never the same two days in a row. Nobody will even recognize me."

Costanza threw up her hands. "You've gone mad. That can be the only answer. You've lost your mind."

Mauro smiled impishly. "You're probably right."

Costanza sipped her wine, one arm folded over the other. Mia could see her fiancée was craving another cigarette.

"What were you even talking about in there?" Costanza asked. "You told the attendant this was a matter of life and death. Life and death? Why would you say that?"

"It's just a turn of phrase," Mauro replied. "Like saying it's raining cats and dogs or that someone has a brain like a computer."

"No, you meant it, Zio. I could see it in your eyes. You meant every word."

Mauro looked away, but Mia could see Costanza's words had left their mark.

"Why here?" Costanza continued. "Why Santa Maria Gloriosa? What hold does this place have over you?"

Mauro took a deep breath, seemingly no longer interested in his food. "It's the casket," he said. "That damn casket."

"What about it?" Mia asked. "I mean, I can see it's quite striking from an artistic point of view, but the casket itself is drab. It's just a black box."

"It's not how it looks," Mauro said. "And the painting behind it is irrelevant as far as I'm concerned."

"Then what?" Costanza asked.

"I need to open it."

Mia almost choked on her wine. "Excuse me? Did you say open it?"

"I need to know who's buried inside it."

"There's a body in there?" Mia asked.

"Remains, yes, but I need to know who those remains belong to."

"Okay," Costanza said. "This really is nuts."

Mauro leaned forward, a look of steely determination in his eyes. "I need to go back to determine how it can be done. I spotted a cherry picker in the corner of the Basilica before I was evicted. It seemed promisingly close to the casket, so if I can just—"

"If you can just what?" Costanza exclaimed. "Steal the cherry picker and somehow place it beneath the casket so you can pry the lid open?"

"Exactly," Mauro replied. "Although I can't make the climb myself, so one of you will have to help me."

"You're actually serious," Costanza said. "In your mind, this is actually a real thing."

"More real than anything I've ever said before."

"But why, Zio? Why is this so important to you?"

"Because my life depends on it. The future of my family depends on it."

"I can't even look at you right now," Costanza said, throwing her hands in the air.

"Maybe if we ask the friar again," Mia said, trying to defuse the terse exchange, which was drawing concerned looks from the other diners.

"We just got banned, remember?" Costanza replied.

"The Venetian archives, then," Mia offered. "I'm sure they might have some helpful advice."

"To rip the lid off a five-hundred-year-old casket?" Costanza scoffed.

"I don't know," Mia said. "I'm just trying to help."

"There's no information about the casket in the Archives," Mauro said. "Trust me, I've already looked."

"Are you sure?" Mia asked. "I mean, I don't want to tread on any toes here, but the Archives have notarized every detail of Venetian life since the creation of the republic. I find it hard to believe that something as striking as the black casket of Santa Maria Gloriosa dei Frari would be omitted."

"Then look if you like," Mauro replied. "But I'm telling you, it's not there."

"So it was missed?" Mia asked.

Mauro shook his head.

"Removed, then?"

"Displaced," Mauro said. "Hidden perhaps."

"But why would somebody do such a thing?"

Mauro glanced at the onlookers behind them, glared at them until they went back to their meals, and then leaned closer, one hand pressed to his mouth. "People in the city have speculated for centuries about who is really in that casket. Some of them believe it's the Count of Carmagnola, a man who was tried and beheaded for treason. What better way to show Venetians how treachery is dealt with than by displaying the criminal's casket in one of the most revered churches in the City?"

Mia was intrigued. "But there's no proof it's him."

"None in the public records," Mauro replied.

"I'm not buying it," Costanza said, holding up her cell phone. "Let's look this up."

"Tsk!" Mauro exclaimed, his anger rising to his cheeks. "Don't you think if it was as simple as asking Google I would have found the answer already? I have been researching this thing for years, my niece, and I can find no evidence either way. Your Aunt Susan and I trawled the records, visited Venice many times, and interviewed dozens of people. There was nothing. Not one shred of proof."

"Susan?" Mia asked. "Your wife?"

Mauro nodded, but she could see he wasn't in the mood to be pressed on the topic.

"I need some kind of answer," he said, his voice steeped in emotion. "We need to open that casket. It's the only way."

Costanza bit down on a mouthful of fritto misto and washed it down with wine. "You seem to be confused, Zio. You just said 'we.'"

"There is safety in numbers, my niece."

"I'm not getting involved in this madness," Costanza said. "I'm not being arrested for opening up the casket of a guy that's been dead for over half a millennium."

"We can just take a look, then," Mauro urged. "See if there's any way this can be done safely without involving the authorities. Just a little peek, that's all we need. I feel sure of it. Once I see what's in that casket, I'll know either way, and then all the years of doubt and uncertainty can be put to bed. Maybe then I will sleep easily. Maybe then—"

"You want us to scramble up some cherry picker in broad daylight?" Costanza asked. "You think that's sane? You think that's a normal thing to ask of your niece and her fiancée?"

"No, not in broad daylight. We can sneak in at night through the cloister."

"You've got to be kidding me," Costanza groaned. "Please, Zio, tell me this is all some kind of poorly-thought-out joke."

"We could even go tonight," Mauro continued. "We could wait until everybody's asleep, until the city is silent and the streets are empty, and do it then. Where's the risk in that?"

"No, Zio, no!" Costanza cried.

"Look," Mia said, noticing the table behind was taking a renewed interest in their heated exchange. "Let's all just calm down a little here."

"Calm down!" Costanza said. "Are you listening to this, Mia? Are you hearing what he's saying?"

"You don't understand," Mauro said. "You've never understood."

"What is there to understand, Zio? You want us to break into one of the most important churches in Venice to open an old box and look at the ashes of someone we don't know, just to satisfy some decades-long research project undertaken by you and Aunt Susan. Have I pretty much summarized what you're asking of us?"

Mauro's face turned ashen. "It's not a research project! I'm going... I want to... I just feel like I have to..."

"Are you okay, Zio?" Costanza said, suddenly looking concerned. "Look, I'm worried about the stress this obsession is putting on your body. I don't want you to have another heart attack."

Mauro grunted, as if the act of forcing out another word was too much for his ailing heart.

"I'm sorry," Costanza said. "But we're not helping you, and that's my final word."

She retrieved a packet of cigarettes from her purse and headed toward the doorway, leaving Mia sitting there alone with her uncle, wondering what to say or do. Mia glanced around the restaurant, looking for a way to break the silence. Mauro slipped a leather bound book toward her.

"Read this when you have a moment," he said, somehow regaining his composure.

"What is it?" Mia asked.

"A journal. A notebook detailing all my research as well as the research undertaken by Susan. It's all in there. Every last thing. Believe me, it's a very interesting read. Someone like you with a background in this kind of thing ought to find it intriguing."

"But Mauro," Mia replied. "Costanza just said—"

"I know what she said," he interjected. "But my niece is like her mother. She's closed off to this kind of thing. You, on the other hand? I could see it in your eyes while we were talking. You have a passion for it."

Mia looked down at the journal, at the dusty cover and the yellowing pages. She had to admit, the contents did interest her. "I don't know."

"If you want to help me," he said, "and I think you do, then meet me at Caffe Floriàn in the morning. Say 8 a.m.?"

He took Mia's hand in his, gripping it a little too tightly, as if by letting her go, he would lose the last vestige of hope he had left. She glanced up at him and could see the desperation in his stare, the anxious tic in his eye. He needed this, and yet she had no idea why.

"Of course," he said, releasing her hand. "If, like Costanza, you decide this is beneath you, then slip the notebook back under my door, and we will never speak of it again."

With that, he placed his napkin on the table, stood, and strode out of the restaurant. Mia just sat there, staring at the book, wondering whether opening it was a wise move, or if just thinking about it was going against what her fiancée had decided.

"Where's he gone?" Costanza asked, returning.

"I... I think he went for a walk," Mia replied.

"Typical. I guess that means I'm paying again."

Costanza looked down at the journal as Mia felt her face flush with heat. "God, did he forget that too?" she asked.

Mia shook her head, scrambling for something to say. "I guess he did."

"Give it to me," Costanza replied, exhaling. "He'd lose his head if it wasn't screwed on so tight."

"I'll do it!" Mia blurted out, afraid the book would be taken from her, and the secrets of the black casket with it. "I mean, I'll give it back to him. You don't need to bother yourself with it."

"Good," Costanza said, raising a hand for the check. "Because I'm done with that uncle of mine for the evening. I just want to go back, have a glass of wine on the balcony, and forget about my zio's crazy ramblings."

Back in their room, Costanza changed into an oversized plain white T-shirt and a black thong. She stood half in the bathroom, half in the bedroom, brushing her teeth with her usual vigor. Meanwhile, she talked to Mia through mouthfuls of foamy, minty paste.

"I can't believe he tried to get you onside, like that," she said. "Waiting until my back was turned and then attempting to recruit you to his maniacal cause."

"It wasn't exactly like that," Mia said, lounging on the bed in her pajamas while browsing through Mauro's book. She hadn't been able to keep the true purpose of the journal from Costanza for long. She had never been great at keeping secrets. Even her own mother said so.

"What, then?" Costanza asked. "It's not like we're on Candid Camera or something. This isn't a joke. Zio Mauro is acting he's like that guy from the Da Vinci Code. What was his name?"

"Professor Robert Langdon," Mia replied, turning another page.

"Yes, that's him. My zio is no Tom Hanks, let me tell you, and you'd do well to forget about these wacky notions of his."

Mia barely paid her any mind. She was too engrossed in the detailed notes and sketches in the journal. Mauro and Susan had gone to great lengths to document a timeline of events, including every shred of evidence that pointed to the casket: painstaking interviews with esteemed historians, Venetian artists, people connected to the Catholic Church, and even descendants of both the count and a man named Alvise Della Torre whose remains were allegedly contained within the casket.

"You're still reading it," Costanza said, poking Mia's thigh with her bare foot. "Are you a glutton for punishment?"

"I find it fascinating," Mia replied. "I must admit, I'm a little curious, too."

"Curious?" Costanza exclaimed. "About some old remains that have been in that box since, what? The seventeenth century?"

"According to what your uncle speculates, the fifteenth century, actually."

"Big deal. What's a couple of hundred years when all you have is dust and old bones?"

Mia laughed. "I think you're saying that to the wrong person, Cos my darling."

Costanza pushed the cushions aside and lay down on the bed, resting her face on Mia's abdomen and wrapping her hands around her back.

"Is this really that important?" she asked.

"Maybe," Mia replied, stroking Costanza's hair. "Maybe not. I just can't get the thought out of my head that the remains in that casket could be somebody else's, and if they are, why?"

"Is that what he thinks?" Costanza asked. "That there's a case of mistaken identity?"

"No, worse than that," Mia replied. "I think your uncle thinks that the remains of Alvise Della Torre were removed, and somebody else's remains were put in their place."

"But why? What possible purpose would somebody have to swap out the body of one person for another?"

Mia's expression darkened. "To hide them, perhaps."

Costanza pushed herself up on her elbows. "This all just seems like a morbid fantasy," she said. "My uncle is chasing conspiracy theories when there's nothing there to find."

"I don't know," Mia said. "It's a little tricky to follow what he says, because his handwriting isn't the best. It took me ten minutes just to decipher that last passage. I find it wild that he still writes his notes half in Italian and half in English. I mean, who does—"

Costanza pressed her lips to Mia's mouth, stopping her fiancée mid-flow. "Shut up," she said. "You're boring me."

"Don't be so rude," Mia replied, half-smiling. "How did your uncle even end up in the US?"

Costanza let out a frustrated exhale. "You want the potted history of my Uncle Mauro? Is that what gets you off?"

Mia playfully slapped Costanza's arm. "Don't say it like that. I'm just interested, that's all."

Costanza flopped back on the bed. "Well, if you must know, he was born and grew up in Milan like Mamma. In fact, he went to the same Polytechnic Institute as both my Mamma and I. He graduated in Architecture."

"A real family establishment," Mia said.

"I guess you could say that. This isn't England. Most people in Italy study in the town they grew up in."

"Except your uncle eventually moved to America."

"After school, yes. He was a very clever student and attracted the attention from a number of universities. One of them was Rice University in Houston, Texas, which offered him a scholarship to complete his master's degree, and while my grandparents didn't want him to travel all that way for his education, my zio thought it was an opportunity too good to miss."

"Why not?" Mia asked. "Something like that must have been really exciting for him."

"I guess it was," Costanza replied. "He must have enjoyed it because he stayed on to gain his master's degree, and from there secured a job at a very prestigious national architecture firm."

"What did he do there?" Mia asked.

"I'm not sure, and my uncle has never been too open about it. I know he was involved in some pretty substantial design projects, but beyond that, I do not know."

"How did he meet your aunt?"

"Susan lived in a different part of Houston," Costanza said. "A very wealthy part. Her family made a lot of money in the oil business, and when Susan's father died suddenly, she inherited a small fortune. From what I can tell, my zio and Susan met at a party thrown for Texan business people and upper class socialites. Mauro asked Susan to dance, and one thing led to another."

"So all of a sudden he was rich."

"Richer than you can imagine," Costanza replied. "But Susan made sure her money remained in her name. She had Zio Mauro sign a pretty watertight prenup to make sure he wasn't just interested in her for the size of her bank account."

"Wise move," Mia said. "Although I'm sure your uncle wouldn't do anything of the sort."

"We're talking big money," Costanza said. "Susan is super rich, and the mansion she shares with my zio, it's gigantic. It's basically a museum. They collect so many historic artifacts, mostly from Italy, some of them older than Christ himself. When we'd visit when I was a kid, I'd walk around like I was on eggshells, terrified I would break something."

"I'm jealous," Mia replied. "I'd love to have a home like that."

"Hey!" Costanza cried. "Listen, I love art too, but the kind of money they were spending on nothing but urns? It was crazy. I'm sorry, but I would never spend tens of thousands of euros on a piece of old clay just because it came from some run-down old ruin in Egypt."

"That is where you and I are different. If I had that kind of money, I'd definitely spend it on art and history."

"So, you'd buy an urn for thirty-thousand euros?"

"Sure, why not?"

"You are crazy."

"No, you're crazy," Mia replied, hitting Costanza with a pillow.

"Hey, that's not fair!" Costanza cried, laughing as she tried to defend herself.

"Anyway," Mia replied, letting the pillow drop to the floor. "I'm trying to read here."

"And I'm trying to cuddle."

"Cuddling can wait." Mia grinned. "This is far more interesting."

"Than me?" Costanza cried. "You'd rather read my zio's boring old notes than make out with the woman you're planning to marry?"

Mia dropped the journal onto the bed and sighed. "I'll slide it under his door tonight if it bothers you so much."

Costanza grabbed the notebook and tossed it onto the floor.

"You're in one of those moods," Mia said.

"There's only one mood I'm in," Costanza said, running her hand down Mia's thigh. "And it's not one where I wish to talk about my family and their crazy ideas."

Mia wrapped her arms around Costanza's neck and drew her in. As they slipped back onto the bed, their lips touched, and their tongues found each other. Mia pulled at her lover's T-shirt, slipping it over Costanza's head, revealing her slim physique and pert breasts. She kicked off her pajamas as they slipped beneath the sheets, tumbling and caressing, her lips finding her lover's neck, her shoulders, the soft flesh behind her ears. She paused, gazing into Costanza's eyes, her desire burning brightly, breathless and unsated, and then she fell onto her, her lust as hot as burning sulfur, her passion like giant waves on a rolling ocean.

She awoke at two in the morning. Costanza was draped across her, her tanned body bathed in milky moonlight that seeped through the open drapes. Mia slipped out from under her, too lost in her own thoughts to sleep any longer. Costanza groaned and reached for her, but in no time at all she fell back into a restful sleep. Mia padded across the floor in bare feet, pulled on her pajama pants, and slipped into a chair in front of her laptop. She opened the screen and logged in, selecting her browser and typing in *Santa Maria Gloriosa dei Frari*. While the computer brought up her search responses, she reached down and collected Mauro's journal, thumbing through the pages as she selected the search response at the top of her screen. There was so much about Mauro's research she wanted to understand, and so much more she wanted to learn.

CHAPTER SIX

VENICE – 1432

The night was dark and silent, as if the whole of Venice were inside some kind of shadow bubble where no sounds existed, and stars were the only source of light. A gondola sailed along the canal, slicing through the still waters like a knife through soft cheese. A woman was on board, straight-backed and graceful, her hands neatly folded in her lap. She was stoic, calm, the only sign of emotion the glistening tears that glowed like drops of silver on her cheeks. The gondolier piloted the vessel along the canals, taking turn after turn until they reached the spot that Antonia Visconti had paid him handsomely to take her to. He rarely worked at this late hour, but the reward for his troubles was more than worth the inconvenience. Even his wife had been happy with him taking on this task, although the woman he was escorting was the spouse of a traitor. What did he care? She hadn't been accused of anything, and the noblewoman had enough money to make any reservations he might have disappear quicker than a gull in flight.

Campo dei Frari loomed up ahead, so the gondolier steered the vessel to the edge of the water, bringing the boat alongside the canal wall before tying it tightly to the cleats. He stepped off the boat and held out his hand, helping the lady onto dry land before accepting the money she slipped him.

"Thank you for your assistance," she said. "The Visconti family will forever be grateful."

"It was no problem, my lady," the gondolier said. "Once again, I am very sorry for your loss."

As the countess crossed the courtyard to Santa Mario Gloriosa dei Frari, he sat down in the shadows, knowing that if anybody saw him, his life wouldn't be worth living.

Antonia Visconti approached the basilica. It was an impressive building that she had visited many times with her husband, and a place she held in great regard. The Visconti family had helped fund much of the renovations in the basilica and continued to be determined supporters. She knew every nook, every aisle. She also knew where all the entrances and exits were, including the side door that she approached now. She had no desire to signal her presence to anyone other than the person she was here to see. Her intentions were singular, her goal as clear as the finest diamond.

She stood before the small wooden opening, took a deep breath, and knocked gently. It wasn't long before the sound of latches being turned came, and the door shifted in its frame. Fra Dolphi appeared in the darkness, his hood pulled over his head like a blackened cowl. Instantly, he glanced up and down the courtyard and lifted a finger to his lips.

"We must be silent," he whispered.

"Then let me in," Antonia replied. "I do not intend to have this discussion out here in the cold."

The friar stood aside and let her enter, and she stood there, letting the chill of the night air leave her bones. She was close to him now, close to the man she was still so madly in love with. He had been taken from her too soon, and for what? To satisfy the egos of men who would cut the throats of their own mothers to satisfy their gluttonous egos.

"Where is he?" she asked.

"Right this way, Countess," the friar replied. "We did the best we could with the time we had. The task had to be done quickly for fear of somebody seeing what we were up to."

"I understand," Antonia replied. "These are dark times. My husband was executed for being good at what he did. I can only imagine what would happen if the doge ever realized I managed to steal my husband's body away and hide it in a place so close to home."

"It doesn't bear thinking about," the friar replied. "Here, this way."

They moved through the basilica in silence as above them the Virgin Mary looked down, watching them pass the altar and head outside to the Chiostro della Vergine. In one corner, beneath a tall arch, a mound of earth looked out of place. It was around six feet long and two feet wide.

"Here?" Antonia asked, feeling the tears coming.

"Yes, he is here," the friar replied, drawing the sign of the cross on his chest.

Antonia dropped to her knees beside her husband, caressing the earth as if he lay atop it, letting the soil slip through her fingers like the sands of time that had been so cruelly taken from them. She let out a long, low sob as the grief seeped through her lips. If only she could have saved him. If only they'd never come back to Venice. There were so many things she would have done differently, so many moments she would have savored if she had known they would have been their last together.

"I'll let you be alone with him for a while," the friar said.

"Thank you," she replied. "For what you have done here. I will be forever grateful."

The friar nodded his acceptance of her thanks and then slipped away, disappearing into the basilica, while overhead, the clouds slid across the moon like the passing of time.

Later, Antonia sat on a bench across from her husband's grave, wanting to spend as much time in her beloved's presence as possible. The friar returned to her and took a seat to her right, his hood lowered, hands folded in his lap.

"I have a confession to make," Antonia said, her voice cold and without emotion.

"We can go inside if you wish. I do not normally take confessions at this late hour, but for you, I will of course make an exception."

"Here will do just fine," she said, waving a hand dismissively. "I just need to say something that's been on my mind."

The friar nodded, made a sign of the cross in the air, and said, "In nomine patris et filii et spiritus sancti. Il Signore sia nel vostro cuore. Perché possiate pentirvi e confessare umilmente i vostri peccati."

The countess paused, taking a few short breaths before speaking. "Is the desire to seek justice a sin, Fra Dolphi?"

"It depends what you mean by seeking justice," the friar replied.

"I mean just that. The man who did this to my husband committed a crime, and for that he should be brought to heel."

"If his crime can be proven, then surely he will be tried by those in power, and he would be punished for his actions."

"Those in power would not see this as a crime," Antonia hissed. "Just as they would never deliver a guilty verdict against one of their own."

"I know not of whom you speak, my lady. Perhaps if you would just—"

"I've changed my mind," Antonia said, clenching her fists. "I don't need to make a confession, because I have yet to commit a sin."

"Very well," the friar replied. "If you're sure."

"I have a request, however," she said.

The friar turned to her. "Anything."

"Be careful what you agree to," she said. "Because my request is something that may not please you."

"What is it?"

Antonia paused for a moment, pondering her next words. "I need a refuge."

"For you? But why? The doge has not decreed that you have committed a crime, and as far as I know, you are still a free woman."

"No, not for me. For justice."

The friar's brow furrowed. "I... I don't understand."

"I want the man who betrayed my husband to be dealt the most severe punishment possible."

"I thought you just said—"

"He must be killed in the most ruthless fashion for what he did to the man I love."

Fra Dolphi held up his hands. "Countess Visconti, I'm afraid we cannot allow that sort of—"

"I am not asking you or your friars to hurt a man, I just... " She looked over at her husband's grave as her eyes once more welled with tears. "I just want a place for his body to be hidden."

The friar shuffled in his seat uncomfortably, looking as though he would rather be any place else. "My lady, as I said, we are a church, and as a man of God—"

"The body will be here within the next two moons at this same late hour," Antonia said, cutting him off. "I would expect that you would honor what I am asking you with the same level of privacy and diligence that you afforded my husband."

The friar's face turned as pale as the moon overhead. "I have been your family's confessor for these many long years now," he said.

"Perhaps too long," she replied.

The friar swallowed. "My lady, the execution of your husband was an unspeakable act for which there are no words. I cannot explain what happened or try to understand what you are going through."

"No, you cannot."

"But please, do not let the darkness that overshadows your family taint the way you perceive right and wrong. Please do not let Satan himself devour you. The only way to maintain some balance in what is a horrific time is to pray, and I ask that you do that with me now." He bowed his head. "Pray, ask for mercy for him, for those who are driven by the evil, for your temptation to sin—"

"I am not interested in words, Fra Dolphi. I want justice. I demand it!"

The friar shook his head, too anxious to speak.

"Let me spell this out in a way you can understand," she said, speaking calmly but with a sternness that punctuated her words. "My family have been benefactors of this church for many years, and your establishment has benefited greatly from our generosity. I would hate for that funding to stop and for the basilica to fall into disrepair. Such a pretty place, such important history. It deserves the best treatment, does it not?"

The friar did not speak. He knew exactly what the gravitas of her words meant, and he knew what would happen if he refused to do what she asked.

"And of course there are the developments," Antonia continued. "Surely you must see that Santa Maria Gloriosa cannot become the most sumptuous church in Venice if it is never completed. It would be a pity if the construction was to halt as early as daybreak."

The friar's expression shifted as the weight of acceptance bore down on him. Antonia knew then that she had him, that he would do exactly what she wanted. Her heart was heavy, but her spirit was buoyed. Her husband would be avenged, and the body of the man who had betrayed them so terribly would never be found. She eyed the patch of earth beneath which her husband lay and whispered him a silent vow. She would not rest until the job was done.

"The Lord is with you," the friar said beneath his breath.

Antonia let his words hang in the air, allowing herself to be embraced by God's one true wisdom as the shadows of night caressed the courtyard.

"Bless the Lord," she said. "Deo gratias."

CHAPTER SEVEN

VENICE – 1964

The boy peered out the window, watching as the station came into view, dozens of passengers waiting to board the train while many more waited to depart. The carriage bustled with life, so many people eager to witness the wonders of the great city. Mauro was too young; he didn't yet know what he was about to see. He only knew that his grandfather was thrilled to be here, and because of that, he was thrilled, too. He loved his nonno almost as much as he loved his parents. His grandfather would always look out for him, buy him treats when his father wasn't looking, and ruffle his hair when he'd been naughty, shooting him a mischievous wink and telling him it would all be okay.

"Are you ready, Mauro?" his grandfather said. "When those doors open, there will be a great rush. I don't want you to get lost in the sea of people."

"I'm ready," Mauro said, gripping his grandfather's hand. He wouldn't get lost. He wouldn't allow anyone to separate him from his nonno.

He looked up at his grandfather's face. His mom always said the two of them were so much alike. Same dark hair, same thin nose and rounded chin, same inquisitive eyes.

"Here it comes," his grandfather announced. "Venezia Santa Lucia. A station built in the thirties when Venice was finally connected to the mainland by a bridge."

As the train clunked to a halt, the doors opened, and Mauro and his grandfather were pushed forward as the momentum of the crowd carried them toward the platform. Outside, dozens more passengers tried to get in, creating a huge human sandwich within which the pair became the filling. Mauro thought for one moment he might get crushed by the onrushing mob, but with one giant haul, his nonno wrenched him free. In an instant, they were standing in the center of the platform, looking back at the melee.

"That was close," his grandfather said, shooting him a wry smile. "Some people don't have any patience."

He led the the young boy to the station door, and in no time at all they descended the steps that led to the Gran Canal. Mauro took in the sights of this wondrous lagoon, the many boats that sailed along it, and the hundreds of people that lined the waterway, standing on the bridges, drinking coffee, chatting eagerly, and devouring rich pastries and hot pizza.

"Welcome to Venice," his grandfather said. "A place that has no equal."

"It's beautiful," Mauro said.

His grandfather smiled, pulling him close as he led him along the water's edge. "This is nothing," he said. "Wait until you see what I have in store for you."

They crossed the bridge, slicing left and right to avoid the onrushing tourists, and headed down a narrow street intersected by a canal. Residential properties loomed over them, mothers and daughters hanging their washing on lines pulled tight across narrow windows, while husbands and fathers stood outside, smoking cigarettes and cleaning that day's catch. They proceeded on, ignoring the restaurants and bars that teemed with life, until his grandfather found what he was looking for: the Basilica of Santa Maria Gloriosa dei Frari.

"This is it," he said to Mauro. "This is what I wanted you to see. Brace yourself, my boy, because you are about to be blown away."

They entered the church, which was bathed in darkness save for a few candles that flickered gently on either side of the nave. His grandfather didn't waste time. He hurried them to the rear of the church and approached a small wooden door.

"Do you see?" he said to Mauro.

Mauro shook his head. "See what, Nonno?"

"Not down there, dear boy," he said, raising his grandson's face. "Up there, high above the door."

Mauro tilted his head until he could see what his grandfather was so excited about. There was a black box above them.

"What is it?" he asked.

"Listen, Mauro," his grandfather said, dropping to his knees so they were approximately the same height. "I don't have much longer to live. I know that sounds harsh, but it's the truth of it, and I always believe the truth tastes less bitter when it's eaten in broad daylight."

Mauro shook his head, still reeling from his grandfather's revelation. "I... I don't understand."

"How could you?" his grandfather replied. "Because your father would never allow me to tell you."

"Tell me what?"

"He said you needed protection, but protection from the truth is no truth at all. I would much rather know if there was a curse hanging over me, because then I would have the ability to perhaps do something about it."

"A curse?" Mauro asked, his eyes widening as he spoke. "What kind of curse?"

"The worst kind," his grandfather replied. "The kind that darkens every doorway and chills every room. The kind that can change a good day into a terrible one and shift a person's fortune so that everything they touch turns to ash."

Mauro found himself increasingly scared and wondering if his nonno had lost his mind.

"You must know what is truly happening, Mauro. I cannot let you live another second longer without understanding the fate that hangs over our family. Do you understand what I'm telling you? Do you comprehend what I'm trying to say?"

Mauro's eyes flitted from his grandfather to the black casket and back again. He wondered what truth was about to be bestowed upon him, and what darkness would be revealed from within the shadowy confines of the basilica.

"Well, let me begin," his grandfather said. "But know this. When I'm done, you will have more questions than answers, because the secrets that hide in Venice are stubborn and canny, and they bury themselves in tiny crevices and shadowy corners. Just when you think the truth is within touching distance, it will evaporate like water, and you will be left wondering whether it was truly there at all."

The next day, Mauro was playing in his bedroom when he heard the sound of two men shouting in the living room. He raced across the hallway and peered inside, fearing the house was being burgled or someone was attacking his father. His heart hammered in his chest as he crouched, peeping through the gap in the door, watching the furious exchange between the two men in his life.

"I told you not to say anything to him," his father said. "Boys are impressionable at this age, and what you told him might scar him for life."

"He needed to know," his grandfather said. "He should have been told a long time ago."

"If anybody was going to tell him, it should have been me!"

"Then why didn't you?" his grandfather replied.

"Because I didn't want to scare him."

"Nonsense! You were too afraid to tell him. You have always been scared of the curse, as if the very act of voicing it would bring it upon you like a scythe."

"You went against my wishes," his father said.

"Because your wishes were a fallacy and your opinions corrupt."

"Is it corrupt to want to protect my child?"

"No, but you shouldn't have wrapped him in cotton. Mauro is a smart kid, and you've been treating him like a baby."

Mauro's father waved a finger at the old man. "How I treat my son is no business of yours!"

"I won't let you deceive him!"

"I have *never* deceived him!"

"That is all you have ever done! This is his family, too! He is an Imperi man, just like you and I, and Imperi men have carried this with them for centuries! To deny such a thing is to deny there is a God!"

"Get out!" Mauro's father yelled. "Get out of my house. I can't even bear to look at you!"

Mauro sat, tears welling in his eyes, wondering whether the argument between the two of them was all his fault. What if he hadn't gone to Venice? What if he hadn't listened to what his grandfather had told him? What if he hadn't told his father all about it when he'd arrived home, still magically enthralled by the black casket and the historical tales his nonno had regaled him with?

As he watched his grandfather leave, and he listened as his dad told his mother how his own father had angered him, he realized this wasn't the last time he would hear about the Imperi curse, or the only time he would wonder what the truth behind the mystery really was.

A little over two months later, a knock sounded on the door. When his father opened it, his cousin stood there, a darkness in his eyes. When Mauro heard what he had to say, the grief took hold of him immediately. His nonno had suffered a massive heart attack and died before the ambulance had arrived. Mauro thought back to the moment in Venice when his grandfather had told him he didn't have long to live. How had he known? Had he predicted his own death?

At the funeral, Mauro stood with his sister, their mother and father either side of them, peering into the grave at his grandfather's casket, knowing that he would no longer be able to spend long afternoons with him, eating cake, drinking soda, and singing along to happy songs on the radio.

As the ceremony ended and each one of the family members tossed a memento into the open grave, Mauro was led back to the house by his father. The young boy could see the hurt in his father's eyes, the regret that gnawed at him. His dad hadn't spoken to his nonno since the fierce quarrel two months earlier, something that Mauro was sure weighed heavily on his heart. He gripped his dad's hand, eager to tell him that none of this was his fault, but unable to find the right words to ease his father's troubled soul.

Back at the house, Mauro's grandmother brought out the food, laying it on the table for the guests to devour. Mauro stood alone by the window, too upset to eat and too emotional to talk.

"Mauro, my boy," his grandmother said, taking a seat beside him. "You look very sad."

"I loved Nonno," Mauro replied, tears slipping down his cheeks. "I'm going to miss him so much."

"I'll miss him, too," she replied, her own eyes welling with tears. "He and I had spent every day side by side since I was just a young girl of sixteen. It feels so strange to wake up in the morning without him lying in bed beside me. It's like there's a hole where he used to be, a piece of the world that's missing."

Mauro nodded his understanding because he felt the same way. He could still smell his grandfather's favorite brand of tobacco and the musky cologne he wore on important occasions.

"I have come over here to ask something of you," his grandmother continued. "You may choose to refuse, but I sincerely hope you do not."

"What is it?" Mauro asked. "If it's something for Nonno, of course I will do it. I'll do anything."

"I know your grandfather took you to the Basilica of Santa Maria Gloriosa dei Frari," she said. "I know he showed you the casket."

"He did," Mauro replied. "He told me about the curse, too, although there were many things he did not know."

His grandmother nodded as she dabbed at her eyes with a handkerchief. "He was obsessed with that place. There wasn't a week that went by without him mentioning it at least once. At first I thought it was romantic, but as the years went on, the very sound of Maria Gloriosa dei Frari made me want to get up and leave the room."

"He was a very persistent man," Mauro said, smiling. "When Nonno got something in his head, he would never let it go."

"And that is why I'm talking to you in private," she said. "As much as that place haunted our marriage like a malignant spirit, your grandfather was getting close to the truth. I would hate to think that whatever it was he was chasing would elude him, even in death."

"You think there's more to the curse than even Nonno knew?" Mauro asked.

"I think there's something about that casket and the mystery that surrounds it that deserves to be unraveled, if only to honor your grandfather's memory."

Mauro stood there, looking down at the frail figure of his grandmother, wondering what secrets lurked just beyond the edges of his understanding. His grandfather had told him so much: stories of medieval lords and counts, of murder and subterfuge, but there was still so much he didn't know. Could he help? Was there a way he could do as his grandmother asked and fulfill his nonno's legacy? He knew if he did, his father would be angry, but if not him, who? Could he really allow all his grandfather's work to go to waste?

"I'll do it," he said, clutching his grandmother's hand. "I'll do as you ask."

The tears came to both of them. Tears of joy, tears of relief, and tears of secrets yet to be uncovered and buried truths that deserved to be heard.

CHAPTER EIGHT
VENICE – PRESENT DAY

Mauro's eyes opened. It was still very early in the day, and the room was bathed in inky shadows. He sat up, the dream of his grandfather's funeral many years ago and the promise he had made to his grandmother still fresh in his mind. He reached for the glass of water by the bedside table, instead finding his spectacles, which he perched on his nose while he found the switch for the lamp. With the room now illuminated by the bulb's yellow glow, he remembered something: his journal and the request he had made of the young British woman.

Wondering what had become of his book, he peered at the door to his room. There was nothing beneath it. Mia still had his notebook, which could only mean one thing: she wanted to help him, just like he had promised to help his nonno all those years ago.

He smiled and placed the glass of water to his lips, drinking greedily as he relished what was to come. This would be a good day. A day to remember.

Mia showered and got dressed as quietly as she could, eager to make sure Costanza didn't see her leave. As she looked down at her sleeping lover, she felt a pang of guilt. Costanza didn't deserve to be deceived like this. She didn't buy into her uncle's stories like Mia did, and why would she? She'd had a lifetime of it, countless years where her aunt and uncle would tell her of what lay there in the mysterious church. Mia, on the other hand, was hearing it for the first time. She relished what was in the journal. There was a magic to it, a history that felt real and unreal all at the same time. She wanted to scratch beneath the surface, to see what was hidden beneath the thin veneer that covered it. To do that, she had to do something Costanza had forbidden—she would humor her uncle Mauro by listening to what he had to say. The very thought of it gave her nervous chills.

She slipped out the door, closing it gently behind her, and headed to the elevator. As she arrived in the downstairs foyer, she gave the concierge a happy wave and headed outside, relishing the heat of the morning sunshine. The courtyard was already busy with dozens of tourists, although she knew that later on there would barely be room to move.

She walked along the lagoon to Piazza San Marco, watching as the boats drifted past and listening to the busy chatter of the people that waited at the water's edge. The place was filled with so much love, so much enthusiasm for the intriguing sights, delicious scents, and intoxicating atmosphere. She wished she could spend a month there—two months—but she knew Costanza would never go for that. Her fiancée was already frustrated by her uncle's demands and irritated by her mother's messages. For her, this weekend away was just another reason for her to stay as far away from her family as possible.

As Mia entered the square, she took in the wonders of the palace, the towering columns, and the gothic-inspired basilica. It would never be less than beautiful to her. She wanted to sit in one of the restaurants all day and just people-watch, soaking up the vibrancy of the city. Instead, she had an appointment with Costanza's uncle, and although staying out there in the piazza would be idyllic, she also wanted to hear what Mauro had to say. Caffè Florian was to her left beneath the arches, and she headed toward it, passing a table where a young couple sat, gazing into each others' eyes as they sipped cappuccinos and shared their fragrant breakfast.

She walked through the door of the cafe and gazed in awe at the intricate paintings and elegant decor. The place shimmered with yellows and golds, while the plush benches and chairs were upholstered with crimson velvet. The tables were topped with marble, the ornate legs made from white steel. Dozens of paintings decorated the walls: an Italian woman seated by a river, beautifully dressed nobility lounging in the sunshine.

A man in a white shirt and dark tie approached, his hair neatly combed, mustache trimmed above his smiling mouth.

"Buongiorno," he said. "How may I help you?"

"Buongiorno," she replied. "I have an appointment with my friend."

"Of course. Are you able to see him?"

Mia scanned the room, looking for Costanza's smartly dressed uncle.

"I see him," she said, gesturing toward a room at the back. Mauro was there, sipping an espresso macchiato, his hand raised.

"Of course, Mr. Imperi," the manager replied. "Please, take a seat and one of my staff will be over shortly. Please, relax and enjoy your visit to Caffè Florian."

Mia headed across the cafe toward the Liberty Room, passing by half a dozen tables, all of them filled with energetic tourists and excited travelers. The doorway to the Liberty Room was open, and inside lay another half-dozen glass-topped tables alongside chairs lined with blue velvet. It was a much smaller room but very intimate, with art nouveau decor, arched ceilings, and glistening mirrors.

"Good morning, Mauro," she said. "I see you got here early."

"They make the finest espresso in the whole of Italy," he replied. "I woke this morning with the taste of it on my tongue."

Mia took a seat, glancing at the menu as Mauro set down his cup.

"You read my journal?" he asked.

She nodded. "I must confess, I couldn't put it down."

"And?"

"I found it intriguing. You and your wife did a fantastic job of pulling so many details together. It must have taken you a lot of time."

"Many years," he replied, puffing out his cheeks. "And a lot of late nights. It is as my grandfather once told me. The secrets of the basilica do not want to be found."

Mia eyed the tray of pastries on the table as a waitress arrived, handing her a freshly made cappuccino.

"I took the liberty of ordering," he said. "I noted that you like cappuccinos. You will not be disappointed with this one. It's as exquisite as their espresso."

Mia held the cup to her lips, enjoying the fragrant aroma and creamy froth of the milk. With every passing second, she came to love Venice a little bit more.

"I am surprised you are drinking coffee," she said. "I would have thought that after a heart attack like yours, caffeine should really be avoided."

"Some things in life are worth taking a little risk for," Mauro replied, taking another sip of his hot drink. "And this is one of those things." He glanced at Mia's bag and the journal that peeked out from within its dark confines.

"I see you brought it with you," he said.

She handed it to him and smiled. "It's a precious document. I wouldn't want to hold onto it any longer than necessary."

"It's intriguing, isn't it?" he said. "The story, I mean. So many dead ends, so many suspicious circumstances."

"I'll confess, it caught my imagination like nothing I have read in such a long time. I do have some questions, however."

"Questions?" Mauro asked.

"Yes. Before I agree to anything, I need to know a few more details."

Mauro took a pastry from the tray and placed it on a small plate. He reached out, handing the plate to her as a smile kissed his lips. "Naturally," he said. "I wouldn't expect anything else from an educated woman such as yourself."

Mia took a bite of the delicious croissant and dabbed her mouth with a napkin. "I noted that some of the pages date back from the fifties. Surely you would have been far too young to have been keeping a journal about the basilica back then."

Mauro smiled, nodding his head slowly. "As you quite rightly say, this journal is a precious document like no other. In fact, it was started by my grandfather before I was even born."

Mia set down her pastry. "I'm so sorry to hear that," she said. "But if this journal was started way back then, that means the investigation has been ongoing for—"

"Three generations?" Mauro asked. "Not quite. It is true that my grandfather started it all, but my father was not of the same disposition. In fact, he would rather the story just fade away like an old photograph than dig any deeper. I, on the other hand, was taken in by the mysterious nature of it, and I took on the challenge of unraveling the secrets that have eluded my ancestors for centuries."

"It seems your grandfather was an important person in your life," she said.

"He was. His passing at such a young age affected me deeply. I was very close to him. The information he shared with me is why I've been traveling to Venice so often. Thanks to Susan, I had access to the Venetian Archives, but with her disappearance, it hasn't been an option I have been able to exercise as regularly as I would like."

"And that's why you need me," she replied, shooting him an impish grin.

"Oh, please don't say it like that," Mauro said, feigning hurt. "I would never impose myself on you in such a way. I will confess, however, that when my sister informed me of your education, I did see an opportunity to recruit somebody with skills that are relevant to my cause."

Mia took another sip of her coffee. "Would you like to tell me what you believe is in the Archives that you haven't been able to access already?"

"Absolutely," Mauro replied, becoming more animated. "As I mentioned to you at lunch yesterday, for centuries and centuries, Venetians have been speculating over this casket, wondering why it is there and who is inside. I traced it down to two theories—theories that have been voiced by many but never truly investigated.

Firstly, a traitor to the Republic who was executed in the fifteenth century, an act clearly orchestrated to show the citizens the consequences of such a betrayal."

"And secondly?" Mia asked.

"A nobleman who was murdered in Venice in the sixteenth century. The evidence seems to lean more heavily toward this second outcome, but there are so many pieces of information missing, I remain skeptical."

"You mean missing from the Archives?"

Mauro's brow furrowed. "I mean there is no evidence that suggests why that man was killed."

Mia ran the information over in her mind. The casket was right there in the basilica, displayed for all to see. How could the truth behind what really happened be so hard to find? Surely there were records. Surely somebody would have notarized the events of that day. Unless, of course, somebody wanted the truth to remain hidden.

"I can see the look of disbelief in your eyes," Mauro said. "But there is something else I have yet to tell you."

"What is it?" Mia asked, her interest now so escalated, she could barely contain herself.

"There is information about this supposed traitor that just doesn't add up. No matter how hard I look or how many hours I spend digging through the scant information I have managed to unearth, the pieces just don't fit together, as if the whole thing is a jigsaw puzzle that's missing one vital piece."

"And that piece is?" Mia asked, her excitement palpable.

"I am close to knowing that," Mauro said. "I am so, so close."

Mia was taken aback. An executed traitor. A murdered nobleman. A set of remains in a black casket that hung 25 feet above the ground. What was she missing? What piece of evidence was Costanza's uncle so close to uncovering?

"I need your help," he said. "I no longer have Susan, and without her questioning me and probing in areas I haven't yet thought of, I am afraid I'm missing something."

"I'm not sure I'm the right person," Mia replied. "I don't have the background that your wife has, or the investigative skills."

"I think you are exactly the right person," Mauro said, placing his hand on hers. "I saw it in your eyes the first time I met you. The need to ask questions. The thirst for knowledge. It is exactly what I saw in Susan the first time I met her."

"I don't know," Mia replied. "It seems—"

"It seems like a fantastic, historical discovery that is just inches from our fingertips," Mauro interjected. "Imagine it, you and me on the precipice of a great discovery, one that the whole of Venice has been pondering for half a millennium. We'd rewrite history, Mia!"

"It sounds exciting," Mia replied. "It really does, and part of me wants to, but I just can't see what I would bring to this. I am barely out of university, and I still have so much yet to learn."

Mauro shook his head. "Nonsense. I need your brain. I need your young mind. I am too invested and fogged up by everything. I swore to my grandmother I would get to the bottom of the story, but I fear that I am heading down a blind alley. I need you to guide me, to help me see what I haven't seen. If I don't succeed in my endeavor, I will never find peace. I will never, ever know what my grandfather was chasing."

Mia stared at her swirling coffee, wondering what Costanza would say if she were with her now. She would scoff, of course, and tell her she was being ridiculous for listening to her uncle's flights of fancy. If she agreed to Mauro's request, she risked annoying her fiancée, perhaps even causing a row that could drive a wedge between them. She worried about that, but she also wanted to know the truth. She'd somehow become as invested as the man sitting in front of her.

"I will compensate you handsomely, of course," Mauro said. "I know you have been looking for work, and weddings are expensive these days. I can assure you that I will pay you well."

He grabbed a napkin from the table, retrieved a fountain pen from his pocket, and scribbled a number that made Mia's eyes widen in disbelief. She had known Costanza's uncle was wealthy, or at least his wife was, but this was beyond her wildest imagination.

"I can't possibly accept that," she said.

"You can and you will," he replied. "I can pay you a deposit right away, and when the work is done, I will transfer the balance. But I must warn you, this will not be easy work. You will be doing things that some might consider risky."

"Such as?" she asked.

"More of that later," he replied. "But for the moment, I must have your answer. Will you help an old man get to the bottom of a mystery he's been pursuing for as long as he can remember?"

Mia glanced at the number on the napkin and then at the man sitting across from her. She wondered what secrets lay in wait for them within the walls of the basilica. It was a mystery she'd barely begun to conceive, but now that she had, could she really pull herself away from it?

"We will be a great team," Mauro said. "I just know it."

As he crumpled the napkin in his hands, she knew in her heart she couldn't refuse. Whichever way she looked at it, things were about to get interesting. She only hoped Costanza would forgive her.

CHAPTER NINE

HOUSTON – PRESENT DAY

Ben Imperi sat at the Steinway piano, trying to master the intricacies of Schumann's Piano Concerto in F major. It was a piece he had been trying and failing to get right for weeks, and he was so close now. If he could just get his left hand to work in tandem with his right on the closing section, he'd have it nailed.

The house he lived in was vast, far bigger than was necessary for just the four of them: him, his father, Mauro; his mother, Susan; and their live-in helper, Consuelo were the only people who resided there. What made it even more cavernous was the fact that his mother had been missing now for 18 months. The space she had occupied was a vacuum, a gaping hole in a world he had once seen as the perfect example of American existence. Sure, he had a better life than most of his friends because his parents were wealthy, but more than that, his mother had taken good care of him. He missed her like he would miss oxygen. If she ever returned, he would play her this concerto perfectly because it was her favorite piece. A part of him hoped that by spending all his time perfecting it, somewhere, fate would see to it that she would come home safely.

"Your lunch is almost ready, Señor Ben," Consuelo called out from the kitchen. "Your favorite—creamy chicken and spinach."

"Sounds delicious," Ben called back. "I can't wait. I'm famished."

"It's the piano, Señor," Consuelo said. "You have been hunched over that thing all morning. I'm surprised you have any strength left in your fingers."

Ben smiled. Consuelo was right. He'd been playing for three hours or more, and his hands and arms ached from the exertion. He pushed back from the piano and headed toward the living room, passing the many historic artifacts his mother and father had collected over the years: a bust of a Roman general that adorned the mantel, a bronze soldier's helmet from Pompeii, a collection of clay pots from Pisa. A series of urns lined the wall of the hallway, some of them so large they reached Ben's chest. The house was a veritable museum, a shrine to his father's homeland. When Ben's friends came over, they would always comment on it, joking that his dad's head was so stuck in the past, he could barely see the present. Ben would defend his dad, of course, because that was what sons were supposed to do. His father had his faults, but he would always be that stable presence in his life. With his mother missing, Ben needed that now more than ever.

As he entered the living room, reaching for the TV remote and heading toward the couch, the doorbell rang.

"I'll get it," he hollered, eyeing the movie on TV, some historic epic depicting a chariot race in Rome.

He walked down the hallway and glanced at the screen on the wall monitor. He didn't recognize the man with the gray hair, goatee beard, and rotund belly that overhung his belt.

"Can I help you?" Ben asked, pressing the intercom.

"Inspector Frank Wallace," the man replied, stooping to speak into the tiny microphone. "From Houston PD. I'm here to speak with your father."

"He's not here," Ben replied, wondering if he should have disclosed that information so quickly.

"I see," Wallace answered. "Well, would you mind if I come inside and ask you some questions?"

Thinking the detective might have some information about his missing mother, he reached for the door. "Hi," Ben said. "Ben Imperi. I don't believe we've met."

"No," the inspector said. "All of my dealings so far have been with your father, Mauro Imperi. May I?" He gestured toward the house.

"Of course," Ben said, stepping aside. "Please, follow me into the living room. Would you like a coffee? Consuelo has just made a pot."

"I'm fine," Wallace said. "Thank you for seeing me."

Ben opened the door to the next room and gestured to the couch. "Please, sit. We can talk in private here. It's only Consuelo and me in the house."

Wallace looked up at the paintings on the wall.

"They're Venetian," Ben said. "Eighteenth century, I think. I'm sure you know by now that my father has a fascination with the city."

"I didn't," Wallace replied. "Interesting."

"He's been there many times over the years, as has my mother."

"And you?" Wallace asked.

"Me?"

"Have you been to Venice?"

"When I was a little kid, but not for a long time," Ben replied. "Now, my studies take up all my time. One day, though. I plan to travel around Europe when I get a chance. Everything about it fascinates me."

"Mm," Wallace said. "I guess I can see the appeal, but me, I'm more of a country guy. Hook me up with a horse and miles and miles of open plains, and I'm happier than a fox in a chicken coop."

"You wanted to ask me some questions," Ben said. "But I have a question for you. Have you found out anything regarding my mother's disappearance?"

"We have a few lines of inquiry we're following up," Wallace replied. "Nothing concrete yet, but these things take time. At this stage, we're still confident we'll get to the bottom of it."

Ben shook his head. Every police report they'd received so far simply said they were following lines of inquiry. When would they get to the end of it all? When would they find out where his mom was?

"I heard about your father," Wallace said. "How is he after his heart attack?"

"Better now," Ben replied. "We were very worried at first, but you know what my father's like. He can't sit still for too long. He gets itchy feet."

Wallace nodded. "And where is he now?"

"As I said, my father loves Venice, and as soon as he came home from the hospital, he booked his next trip."

"His next trip?"

Ben laughed. "That's right. He's back in Italy in the city he loves."

"Is that wise?" Wallace asked. "To fly all that way when he's just survived a near fatal cardiac arrest?"

"My father said it was nothing to worry about," Ben said. "And even if I wanted him to stay, he's his own man, and he does what he wants. I have more than enough to keep me occupied here, believe me, and Consuelo is excellent company."

"But Venice?" Wallace exclaimed. "It's such a long way. What if he has a repeat of his health scare?"

Ben shook his head. "You have to realize that since my mom disappeared, my dad's been worried out of his mind. I think the heart attack was just a culmination of everything that's been going on, so when he said he wanted to go, I thought it was a good idea. He's never happier than when he's in Venice, so in my view, this is good for him."

Wallace sat back on the couch. "You know, I think I might have that coffee after all."

"Sure thing," Ben replied. "Consuelo, could you make two coffees? One for me, and the other for the inspector."

Within a few moments, Consuelo appeared with two steaming mugs. She set them down on the table, smiling as she passed the police officer. "I hope you like it," she said.

"Gracias," Ben replied.

"Yes, gracias," Wallace added, raising the cup to his lips. "I'm sure it's lovely." The inspector eyed the room. "You have a lot of antiques," he said. "An unusually vast collection."

"My father's idea," Ben replied. "And my mom, she knows what she's looking for. These items come from all over Italy. Some of them are worth tens of thousands of dollars. My mom was always complaining about the impact my father's spending had on her bank account."

Wallace puffed out his cheeks. "Somebody would pay tens of thousands for items that are hundreds of years old? Maybe I should sell my own record player," he said, setting his cup down. "I bought it for ten dollars back in the eighties. Maybe that would be worth something."

"Depends on the vintage," Ben replied. "And on the manufacturer. If my mom was here, perhaps she could have advised you."

Wallace shrugged, turning his attention to Consuelo. "It really is nice," he said. "The coffee, I mean."

"Gracias," she replied. "It's a family recipe."

"Whatever it is, I'd pay good money for it."

Consuelo laughed and turned to head back to the kitchen.

"My mom's dead, isn't she?" Ben asked.

"Ben!" Consuelo cried. "You must never say that."

"You can't draw those sorts of conclusions," Wallace replied. "Not until we have something to go on."

"It's been a year and a half, Inspector. What other conclusion am I supposed to reach? Surely if she was still alive, you would have found her already."

"Don't upset yourself like this," Consuelo said, rubbing Ben's back affectionately. "The Inspector will find her, sí, Inspector? It is only a matter of time."

"That's another reason I came to speak to your father," Wallace replied. "It's such a shame he's not here."

"You can tell me," Ben said. "I know I'm young, but with my father out of the country, I'm the man of the house."

Wallace looked down at the floor and nodded. "Okay, well then, I have to tell you that in less than six months I plan to retire. It's a little early, but my boss has sanctioned it, and I've been doing this job for so long, I can barely remember who I was before. My point is, it's time for me to hang up my hat, and if the case isn't solved before then, there's every possibility it may go... cold."

"Cold?" Ben asked. "What does that even mean?"

"It will remain open, but if we don't find any significant leads before I go, it will be considered shelved. Resources will be pulled, and the file will be placed on indefinite hiatus."

Ben shook his head. He couldn't believe what he was hearing. "Hiatus? But she's still out there somewhere. Even if she's dead, surely you have a responsibility to get to the bottom of this?"

"And we will," Wallace said. "I'm confident of it, but I would rather you know every possible outcome. I owe you and your father that much."

"But even so, you would retire rather than find a woman you have been looking for for over a year? You know she hasn't been kidnapped, because if she had, there would have been a ransom demand already. I mean, just look at this house. There is more than enough here to satisfy any kidnapper, so that can only mean one of two things. Either she ran away from us, which she would never do because she loves us, or—" Consuelo tried to hug him, but he shook her off. "Or... she's dead."

"No!" Consuelo cried. "The Inspector is right, niño. You need to maintain faith."

"And where has that gotten us?" Ben asked. "Honestly, at this point I'd rather not know what happened. As absurd as it may sound, I am starting to find some solace in the ambiguity of it all."

"Ambiguity can be comforting," Wallace replied. "But it's no way to live. Look, I know I came here to tell you of my pending retirement, but I still have plenty of time to solve this. I'll give you the same promise I gave to your father. I'll leave no stone unturned, I'll chase down every lead, and I'll work every hour I have left to find your mom."

Ben turned his head, too angry to respond.

"I'll give your father a call and tell him personally, of course," Wallace added. "I owe him that much."

"You own my family much more than that, Inspector."

Wallace stood up to leave.

"I'll show you out, Señor," Consuelo said.

"I wouldn't bother calling him," Ben said, trying to mask his contempt. "He hardly ever answers the phone when he's over there."

"The hotel, then," Wallace said. "Do you know where he's staying?"

Ben checked his phone for the last message his dad had sent him. "The Hotel Danieli, I believe," he replied. "But like I said, he hardly ever calls back."

"I'll give it my best shot," Wallace replied. "Have a good day, Mr. Imperi."

Ben didn't reply. He was too hurt to say anything. He just watched the Inspector leave, wanting so badly for him to turn around and tell him he'd found his mother, but knowing in his heart that hope was dwindling with every passing moment.

Wallace sat at his desk, running the discussion with the Imperi boy over in his head. There were so many things that didn't make any sense to him, so much that was out of context with a man mourning the disappearance of his wife.

"What's on your mind, big guy?" the sub-inspector on his team, Vela, asked. Vela stood to take over when he retired.

"I wish I could tell you," Wallace replied. "I'm still trying to piece it all together."

"This is the Imperi case, right? The case of the missing woman?"

"That's the one, the same case I've been working for longer than I care to think about."

"You went over to see the husband?"

Wallace shook his head. "The guy's out of town."

Vela's eyes narrowed. "Didn't he just have a heart attack?"

Wallace nodded.

"And yet he decided to take a vacation?"

"To Venice."

"Venice, California?"

Wallace shook his head once more, tapping his pen against the desk. "I wish. No, Mr. Imperi decided to catch a plane to Italy."

Vela laughed. "You're kidding, right?"

"Nope. He's there right now, and you should see his place, too. It's like a museum. There are so many historic Italian artifacts dotted around the place. I figure he and his wife must have spent over a million dollars putting that little collection together."

Vela puffed out her cheeks. "That's the kind of money that attracts attention."

"From all the wrong people." Wallace nodded, thinking exactly the same thing.

"You think she's been kidnapped?"

Wallace shrugged. "The kid made a good point. If she had been taken for the money, where's the ransom note?"

"Maybe the kidnappers are biding their time. Or maybe they're waiting to see if her husband makes some kind of move."

"Like going to Venice, Italy?"

"Perhaps," Vela replied. "Stranger things have happened before. Anyway, why do you care about this case so much? Surely you've got better things you could be doing?"

"Like retiring?" Wallace asked.

Vela smiled. "Well, I don't like to admit it, but I'm starting to think about this desk you have by the window, and how much nicer than mine it is."

"All in good time," Wallace replied, pushing his pen into the pocket of his jacket. "I still have some digging to do before I hand in my badge."

Vela peered down at his computer screen. "Since when do you use Instagram?" she asked.

Wallace studied the face of the young British woman on his computer, a lady named Mia Fletcher. She was standing by the side of another woman, Costanza Genovese, with the Venice skyline in the background.

"I did some research," Wallace replied. "The Italian woman is Mr. Imperi's niece, and the British lady standing next to her is her fiancée."

"What has that got to do with the case?" Vela asked. "Do you suspect one of these women?"

"No, not at all," Wallace replied. "But, you see, they traveled with Imperi to Venice, and that view is from their hotel window. Imperi's son told me they were staying at Hotel Danieli, and this seems to back up his story."

Vela nodded. "I got it. So you're trying to figure out why they're there?"

Wallace shook his head. "Not exactly." He pulled his passport from his desk drawer and collected the bag from beneath his desk. "I wanted to make sure the hotel room I was booking was close to theirs."

Vela's eyes widened. "You're going to Venice?"

"Tonight. You wanna come?" he asked, smiling.

Vela grinned, unable to take her eyes off the stunning view from the attractive pair's hotel window. "I wish I could, my friend," she replied. "I wish I could."

CHAPTER TEN

VENICE – PRESENT DAY / NORTHERN ITALY – 1300S

Mia took a bite of her pastry and set it down on her plate, her own notebook on the table as she studied Mauro's face. She'd never seen someone so alive, so engaged by his own single-minded objective. It was as if Venice made the man younger, like the city's aura somehow soothed the effects of his passing years and aging heart.

"Tell me more about the history of the story," she said. "I want to know everything you know."

"Are you sure?" Mauro asked. "There's a lot to tell."

"I'm sure."

Mauro raised a hand and ordered an espresso and a cappuccino. "Where would you like me to begin?" he asked.

Mia smiled. "From the only place that counts. The beginning, of course."

Mauro leaned forward, his elbows on the table, hands folded beneath his chin. "In that case, let me take you back to the fields around Carmagnola, a municipality on the outskirts of Turin, Northern Italy, in the late fourteenth century..."

The fields of Carmagnola contained perhaps some of the most picturesque landscape in the region. The rolling hills teemed with wildlife, so many crops, dozens of varieties of wild flowers and shrubs. Overhead, finches, swallows, and bee-eaters fluttered past, swooping to catch bugs on the wing, diving toward the tall grass, raking the peaks that waved from side to side in the breeze. Tall trees lined the hill's summit, while a smattering of houses overlooked the valley.

Francesco Bussone carried heavy bags of wheat back to his cart, the horses shuffling impatiently on the dirt track.

"Steady now," Francesco said. "We won't be long."

He turned back to the pile of bags they'd harvested, only to see his father clambering in the brambles, picking berries and collecting them in a hessian bag that hung over his shoulder.

"Dad, what are you doing?" he hollered.

"These are too juicy to leave," his father said. "Don't worry, we have time to spare."

"The horses are growing restless."

"Then feed them," he said. "We have time."

Francesco huffed and emptied a sack onto the ground, watching the two animals lapped up the hay, chewing and munching as if their lives depended on it.

In the distance there came a rumbling sound, as if a storm was approaching. Francesco looked up, his hand on the horse's flank, and spied the long line of soldiers approaching from the east. They were dressed in orange, green, and red clothes—large, loose pants that were tied under the knee, their shirts oversized and bulging. The soldier in front carried a crossbow, the soldiers behind brandishing molded wooden sticks with intricate designs. A short, stocky man walked ahead of them. He had the look of someone supremely confident and with the authority and rank to lead this small army. He was wearing a bright shirt and orange tights, and a pair of leather boots that reached just above his ankles. His hat was large, with a long blue feather that fluttered in the breeze. A short sword hung from his waist, its hilt gleaming in the morning sunshine.

As they approached, Francesco glanced at his father, who was rushing to his side.

"Who are those people?" Francesco asked.

"Mercenaries," his father huffed. "Nothing but vicious thugs who would sell their own mothers to fill their purses with coins."

"They look impressive," Francesco replied. "Look at their clothes, their weapons."

"Don't be fooled," his father hissed. "A pig in a silk dress is still a pig."

As the mercenaries drew closer, Francesco saw them more clearly. The men looked well-trained and powerful, and their leader looked like a nobleman, his clothes made with the finest material and his boots with the best leather.

"Why are they even here?" he asked. "I've never seen them before."

"From what I hear, the town hired them to protect the man in charge of Carmagnola, the Count of Saluzzo," his father replied. "But I must confess, it seems a little suspicious to me."

"What do you mean?" Francesco asked.

"Think about it. When have you heard of a nobleman spending money on a militia just to protect what he has?"

"You think this army is an occupying force?" Francesco asked.

His father nodded. "In my opinion, the count plans to expand his territory beyond these borders, not simply consolidate his rule."

Francesco thought about that. There was something thrilling about a force that was so powerful, it could take control of countless towns. The men approaching certainly looked capable, and the man at the head of the procession appeared to have the determination and ruthlessness to lead them to dozens of victories.

"Drunkards, all of them," his father said, his tone spiteful and angry. "There's not one ounce of intelligence in those thick heads of theirs."

"Surely what they do is better than this!" Francesco exclaimed. "Breaking our backs in the sun every day for a few bags of hay and just enough fruit to fill our mouths."

"If puffing out your chest and bragging about how many towns you've pillaged is what you mean, son, then I'd rather snap my back in half."

Francesco stood there, ignoring his father's cynicism and watching the soldiers march by. He felt something inside him, a kinship he'd never felt before. He'd thought his whole world was walking these fields, plowing the earth, and carrying sacks so heavy he barely had the strength to get out of bed in the morning.

What if there was more? What if there was a life beyond Carmagnola?

"Come on," his father said. "Your mother will be waiting with dinner."

Francesco took the reins of the horse and called for it to move. He silently wondered if the thoughts in his head were just flights of fancy, pipe dreams that had no place in the heart of a man like him. Nobility was nobility, after all, and he was just a lowly peasant boy who deserved nothing more than a life of hard labor and servility.

"You, boy!" the man at the head of the militia called out. "You, with the horses and cart!"

Francesco looked up, wondering who this enigmatic captain-general was yelling at.

"Me?" he asked, pointing to his own chest.

"What are you doing?" his father said. "Don't address him. Men have been killed for less."

"Yes, you," the captain-general said. "Come here. Let me look at you more closely."

Francesco felt his heart leap in his chest.

"Don't go to him," his father said, but Francesco was already moving, handing his father the reins as he climbed the hill.

"Do you know who I am?" the captain-general asked.

Francesco shook his head. "Only that you were hired by the town to protect the count," he replied.

The captain-general laughed, turning to the others in his troop who all joined in. "Is that what your father told you?" the captain-general asked. "Well, I suppose it is a truth of sorts."

Francesco felt himself blushing, embarrassed by the sounds of the militia's scorn.

"I am Facino Cane," the man continued. "And these are my men. The finest men in the whole of the region."

The soldiers whooped their reply.

"Do you work these fields?" Cane asked.

Francesco nodded. "Yes, they are my father's. We come out here every day."

"To collect fruit?" Cane asked, clutching a handful of berries from the cart and slipping them into his mouth.

"That and other things."

Cane spat out the pips and wiped his chin with the back of his hand. "I guess it's a life," he said, sneering. "If that's the sort of life you desire."

"It's the only life I know," Francesco said. "I've been doing this ever since I was a young boy."

"A hired hand, that's all you are."

"As are you," Francesco shot back, drawing gasps from the gathered mercenaries.

Cane glared at him for a moment, his eyes filled with rage, but then his expression softened. "Defiance," he said. "I like it. You have no fear."

"Only of that which I do not understand," Francesco said. "But I understand you."

"Really?" Cane replied. "Then tell me, what is it you think you know about Facino Cane and his army of mercenaries?"

"That you kill and plunder," Francesco offered. "That you are ruthless and show no mercy. That you would sack the very town you grew up in if you thought it would bring you fame and riches."

Cane turned to his soldiers, who were anxiously watching to see how this exchange would play out, but when he turned back to Francesco, he was laughing. "You are a perceptive young man," he said. "Smart, too. I could use someone like you alongside me."

"Sorry," Francesco replied, glancing at his father. "I already have a job."

"You want to stay in a shithole like this?" one of the soldiers cried. "The captain-general is offering you a life of wealth and notoriety. You would turn that down for a job that pays peanuts and requires you to toil and slave under the boiling sun?"

"He's right," Cane said. "You are so much better than this."

"Thanks very much," Francesco's father muttered beneath his breath.

"You would have your son follow in your footsteps rather than better himself?" Cane spat back. "What is your name, boy?" he asked, turning back to the young man.

"Francesco," he replied. "Francesco Bussone."

"Then what say you, Francesco? Is this something you think you could do? Do you have the stamina for it? The guts? The passion, the resilience, the strength?"

Francesco eyed the captain-general and considered his request. Could he do it? Should he? Was this a life he could commit to in the way Cane wanted him to? Could he travel the land, fighting battles with the men at his side, conquering towns, overthrowing regimes? Was he the kind of man who could do these things time and time again?

He pondered, he considered, and when he'd run every scenario through his mind, he turned to the captain-general and said...

"I don't get it," Mia interrupted. "What has this young farmer boy got to do with the casket? I know you said you would take me back to the beginning, but nothing about this story seems relevant."

"Give me time," Mauro replied, taking a bite from a slice of cake. "For a story to truly mean something, you have to understand the context."

"I understand," Mia said. "But this context seems entirely out of place. These events you are describing, they didn't even occur here in Venice."

Mauro wiped crumbs from his lap. "And neither should they," he said. "Because our hero did not hail from here. He hailed from the west in Carmagnola."

"I still don't get it," Mia replied. "Are you saying this is the man in the box nailed to the wall of the basilica?"

"Perhaps," Mauro replied. "Because Francesco Bussone had a long career ahead of him after he met Captain-General Cane."

"A career?" Mia asked. "As an expert farmhand?"

"No!" Mauro cried, attempting to stifle his amusement. "Mia, I thought you were a skilled historian. Bussone became the Count of Carmagnola, one of the greatest ever commanders of the Venetian army."

Mia's cheeks flushed pink. "Of course," she said, rolling her eyes. "I hadn't made the connection. He's the man you refer to in the journal, the traitor who was executed by the republic."

"That's right," Mauro said. "And there is every possibility his remains are in that casket. It's just never been proven."

Mia nodded along. "So he accepted Cane's offer."

"Oh, he did so much more than that," Mauro replied, leaving a healthy tip on the table as he stood to leave. "If you'd like to take a stroll with me, Mia, I can tell you the rest of the story."

"The rest of it?" she replied, gathering her things. "There's more?"

Mauro grinned. "You wouldn't believe how this story unfolds."

CHAPTER ELEVEN

VENICE – PRESENT DAY / NORTHERN ITALY – EARLY 1400S

The pair of them left Caffè Florian and crossed the square, walking in the direction of the Bridge of Sighs. Mia had to quicken her pace to keep up, such was the urgency of Mauro's strides. He spoke as he walked, using his arms to express high points and his face to emote feelings. Mia took it all in, scribbling notes as she walked, and attempting as best she could not to fall over or walk into people.

"Much to his father's protestations, Francesco accepted Cane's gracious offer and trained rigorously with the other soldiers, learning both swordcraft and the art of war..."

Over the next twelve years, Francesco became not only a man, but a highly effective warrior who drew plaudits from all those who encountered him. He walked side by side with Cane, shared in some of the captain-general's most famous victories, and gained the respect of his peers. It was said that nobody could outthink Bussone, and that his military prowess was second to none.

Cane grew fonder and fonder of this man he had met in the fields of Carmagnola, and as the years went past, he grew to look at him as a son. Cane himself was getting too old for some of the more challenging skirmishes, and he relied on Bussone to be his eyes and ears on the battlefield, reporting back to him when the battle had been won. Bussone began to take charge of recruitment, military strategy, and punishing anyone who refused to bow to Cane's will.

Bussone ceased being known by his father's name, and instead took on the title of Carmagnola. It was there, after all, where his life had truly taken a turn for the better.

With Cane's army gaining more and more fame, their exploits drew the attention of one of the most influential families in Milan. The Viscontis were politically powerful in the region and were rich patrons of the arts and schools. With one of the family's youngest members, Filippo Maria Visconti, being bestowed the castle and lands of Pavia, a town that resided on the river Ticino in the south of Milan, the Viscontis hired the mercenaries to protect their son's territories. What followed was a long and fruitful relationship that ultimately led to an even greater leap in Carmagnola's fortunes.

One night, after Carmagnola had been summoned to the castle, Facino Cane's guard-in-waiting requested that he visit with the captain-general.

"He is in his chambers," the guard said. "He says he must speak with you immediately."

"Is he unwell?" Carmagnola asked.

"I cannot say," replied the guard. "Only that he requests your company."

Believing his boss to be in some distress, Carmagnola moved speedily to Cane's chambers, only to find him lying in bed with his wife, Countess Beatrice Lascaris, by his side.

"You wished to speak with me," Carmagnola said while trying to catch his breath.

"I did," Cane replied, his own breathing labored, his face as white as milk. "Please, sit."

Carmagnola took the chair across from him and watched as the countess dabbed a cool napkin on Cane's pallid complexion. The noble woman had been a great asset to Cane for many years, and her wealth and social standing had helped him rise to his lofty heights.

"We have received some bad news," Cane said, his voice ragged and coarse.

"Bad news?" Carmagnola asked.

"I'm afraid that Duke Gian Maria Visconti has been murdered."

"Murdered?" Carmagnola exclaimed. "But how?"

Cane waved a hand dismissively. "None of that is important for now. The good news is, this opens up a wonderful opportunity for you. As you know, Filippo Maria is the true Visconti heir, and with the duke out of the way, we can help establish him as the one true Lord of Milan."

Carmagnola's eyes narrowed. "But what has this to do with me?"

"I want you to be the one to protect Filippo Maria, Carmagnola. With his power established, you will lead the greatest army in Northern Italy."

Carmagnola's heart beat faster at the very mention of commanding his own men.

"But what about you, my lord?" Carmagnola replied. "Surely you will be the man to take charge of this powerful army."

"I am afraid not, my friend," Cane replied. "My mind is still sharp, but my body is failing. I have tried to ignore the signs for so long, but Father Time has caught up with me. I don't have the strength, nor the energy, to fight another battle. You must take up this mantle, Carmagnola. You must continue what we have fought so hard to achieve."

Carmagnola felt the excitement coursing through his body, but he felt mixed emotions. Facino Cane had been the one to rescue him from a life of obscurity and thrust him into the spotlight, and yet here he was, a frail old man who no longer had the muscle to lift his sword.

"I am afraid I don't have the strength to give you any more details," Cane added. "And so I asked the bishop to spend some time with you."

Carmagnola turned to see a man in splendid robes standing beside the door. He had dark hair and steadfast eyes.

"Good day, Carmagnola," he said. "I am Bishop Bartolomeo Capra, and I am here to tell you everything I know about the emerging situation in Milan."

Carmagnola had indeed heard of this man of the Church. He was much more than a bishop. If the rumors were to be believed, he was a politician in the pocket of the Viscontis and would do anything to maintain his power and influence.

"Then speak," Carmagnola replied. "I wish to know more."

"As far as we can ascertain," the bishop said, "the duke was ambushed by a group of nobles led by Estore Visconti, a distant relative of Gian Maria. It is said that Estore sees himself as the legitimate heir to the Visconti throne, and his attack on the duke was motivated by greed. He and his men ambushed the duke as he exited his palace, cutting him down like nothing more than a wretched animal. His people have proclaimed Estore as the ruler of the city, but this is not to our liking."

"Because Filippo Maria is a friend of ours," Carmagnola said.

"That's right, and because he is malleable. If we restore him as the rightful ruler, it is likely our relationship with him will blossom."

Carmagnola knew the strategy well. If they showed Filippo Maria loyalty, then the city of Milan would become a territory they could exploit. He also knew that with Cane's health failing, they needed a strong ally to help maintain their influence in Northern Italy. This could be just the boost they needed.

"Then tell me what you want me to do," he said. "I'll do whatever you ask."

As he stood to leave, he heard a gasp from the bed, and looked up to see Cane's body in the countess's arms, his chest no longer rising and falling. There were tears in the countess's eyes as she hugged his body to her. Carmagnola stood there, shocked and speechless. He was on his own now. Whatever came next, he would no longer have his friend and ally by his side.

He kissed his fingers, placed them on Cane's heart, and bid a silent farewell. He would honor this man. He would do everything in his power to ensure their legacy would never be forgotten.

With the countess and the bishop forming a powerful alliance that gave them rule over Cane's remaining army, Carmagnola rode to

Milan where he stood side by side with Filippo Maria. They amassed a force of many hundreds and led them to the city's gates, hollering and demanding that Estore Visconti yield and let them in.

"Will he do it?" Filippo Maria asked. "Will he bend to my will?"

Carmagnola pulled his horse alongside the Visconti heir, his armor gleaming in the morning sunshine. On his helm, there was a large blue feather that wafted in the slight breeze.

"He'll do exactly as we ask," Carmagnola replied. "Because if he does not, we will tear down the city, brick by brick."

As the army grew silent, their many numbers preparing for a long and fierce battle, the gates of Milan slowly opened, revealing dozens of terrified soldiers who knew they were outmanned.

"Very well," Filippo Maria said, looking relieved, and he and Carmagnola led the army into the city where hundreds of locals cheered and waved.

"Carmagnola!" the army began to chant. "Long live Carmagnola!"

With the army occupying the city and punishing anybody who did not bow to Filippo Maria's rule, Estore Visconti fled along with his conspirators, and within a matter of days, Filippo Maria was crowned the Duke of Milan. For Carmagnola, however, the work had just begun. There were many people who would seek to overthrow the new duke, and many nobles who would claim Milan as their own. Filippo Maria knew this and duly appointed Carmagnola as head of his military forces, and for the next few years, Carmagnola led his men to many bloody battles, all of them victorious. His military prowess was put to the test, but he stood up to the challenge, and before long, everybody was bowing down beneath the weight of his mighty sword. With Alessandria, Pavia, Como, and Lodi falling to his army, the duke rewarded him with more gold than he could ever spend, and a splendid castle in the center of the city.

With his fame spreading far and wide, the duke and his advisers grew nervous. Carmagnola was now the second most powerful man in Milan, the highest noble being the duke himself. Bishop Bartolomeo Capra was the man who pointed out to the duke that a stronger alliance with Carmagnola could only help his cause.

"And how do you plan for me to achieve that?" the duke asked. "Everybody loves him, and yet I stand here in the darkness, watching Carmagnola receive adulation usually reserved for nobility."

"A wedding," the bishop replied, a wry smile on his lips.

"A wedding?" the duke asked. "With whom?"

The bishop nodded toward a beautiful woman standing by the window of the palace who was looking out on the crowd below. She had long dark hair, a smooth complexion, and eyes that could soften the hardest of souls.

"Your cousin, Antonia," he replied, watching as the woman turned and departed. "She would make a perfect match for this farm boy from the fields of Turin."

The wedding was a glorious affair, with nobles from all over the region in attendance. The bride, Antonia, was a sight to behold in white silk that flowed to the floor, and Carmagnola, dressed in a suit of armor, was every inch the dashing man. They gazed at each other across the altar, the two of them so clearly infatuated with each other. It was a union made by God, a beautiful conjoining of strength and nobility. When the vows were read out, Carmagnola took his wife in his arms and kissed her tenderly, and she in turn wrapped her arms around him, their bodies pressed together.

That night, the court of the palace was filled with music and dancing, while the bishop watched on from the shadows, hands folded at his waist, his expression portraying the satisfaction he felt at seeing his plan come to fruition.

"It worked," Filippo Maria said to him.

"It did indeed," the bishop replied.

"You can wipe that smug look off your face," the duke countered. "We're yet to see whether this union of yours will bear any fruit."

"Oh, it will," the bishop said, eyes fixed on the young couple. "Of that I have no doubt."

CHAPTER TWELVE

VENICE – PRESENT DAY

Mia's phone rang, snapping her out of the exotic, enticing imagery painted by Mauro's learned words.

"I'm sorry," she said. "It's Costanza. I think I should probably take this."

"Of course," Mauro said, taking a seat by the canal as a washing line fluttered gently overhead. "I need a moment anyway."

Mia turned from him, walking toward the bridge and placing the phone to her ear. "Morning, sweetheart," she said, sounding less than convincing.

"I overslept," Costanza replied. "I didn't set an alarm."

"That's no problem," Mia said. "You're on vacation, after all."

"I know, but I never sleep in this long."

"Honestly, it's fine," Mia replied. "Sleep as long as you want."

Constanza gave a long yawn down the line, then asked, "Where are you, anyway?"

Mia took a moment to compose herself. "I'm out here taking a stroll with your uncle Mauro."

"Aw, bless you. That's so kind. How is he today?"

"A little better, I think," Mia said. "We've had coffee and breakfast, and now we're walking along the canal."

"Is he talking about—"

"The casket? Yes," Mia said. "He's been filling me in on its history, as well as the backgrounds of some of the major players in the story."

"Does he never stop?" Costanza exclaimed, her frustration spilling over.

"I don't think so." Mia laughed, but her anxiety tainted her words. "That is actually something I wanted to talk to you about."

"About my uncle's irritating ways?"

"Sort of," Mia replied, choosing to cut to the chase. "I accepted his offer."

"You did what?"

"I know that's not something you want to hear, but you have to understand, Cos, this is the kind of thing I was trained to do."

"You mean you were trained to humor an old man's misguided whims by chasing after a ghost that has evaded the authorities for hundreds of years?"

"But there's something there," Mia said. "I know there is."

"All you're going to find is a casket full of ash and a whole boat-load of trouble."

Mia shook her head. "He's offered to pay me a lot of money, Cos. Much more money than I'd earn waiting tables or serving drinks."

"There isn't enough money in the world that would make this crazy situation any less painful."

"You didn't see the number he wrote on the napkin," Mia replied. "It was enough to make my eyes water."

"A hundred thousand euros! A million euros! Two million! It doesn't matter. Don't you see? Once he has you on his hook, he will never let go. You'll forever be as invested in this madness as he is, and even if you want to get out, you won't be able to."

"But don't you see?" Mia replied. "Even if this goes nowhere, it will be a great distraction for him. Without this, what does he have? You said yourself, the disappearance of his wife probably contributed to his heart attack. If he has this investigation in his life, then maybe, just maybe, his health will improve."

"It sounds like you're proposing to feed his insanity," Costanza spat back. "And that can't be a good thing. Just look what happened to my Aunt Susan."

"But this could actually go somewhere," Mia replied. "We could make an important discovery through this work. Just think about that, Cos. Think about what that might mean for my career—what it might mean for us."

"Just listen to yourself!" Costanza yelled down the line. "Do you hear how you sound? You're actually starting to sound like him!"

Mia held the phone away from her ear. "I won't speak to you if you're going to lose your temper," she said. "I'm trying to do a good thing here. He's your family, remember, not mine."

"And as a member of his family, I ask you not to do this. This is just bad on so many levels."

Mia chewed her lip. She knew Costanza was trying to protect her, but she was more than capable of protecting herself. And besides, this project was so tantalizing. She hadn't stopped thinking about it ever since Mauro had handed her the journal. There was just something about it that had her in its grasp.

"Just go and take a shower," she said. "Cool off a little. If you want, we can talk about this later."

"And when we do, my dear," Costanza replied, "I'll take you straight back home where my uncle can't get his claws into you."

Mia blew a raspberry down the phone and hung up, no longer happy to carry on the conversation. She loved her crazy Italian fiancée more than life itself, but sometimes she could drive her as crazy as a loft full of bats. Where did she get off trying to protect her when she was her own woman, with her own sensibilities, and her own interests and ideas? If she wanted to help out Mauro Imperi, then she would, and nobody was going to stop her.

She headed back to the bench where Mauro was sitting, dabbing his face and neck with a napkin. She took a seat next to him and breathed in the fresh air. They sat that way for awhile, just watching the world go by as the many residents and tourists walked past, each of them engaged in their own thoughts and conversations.

After a while, Mauro let out a heavy sigh.

"Are you okay?" Mia asked. She had a thought—what if Mauro had heard the conversation she'd just had with his niece? "You didn't... happen to hear any of that, did you?"

"What? Your phone call? No, of course not. I'm not the kind to eavesdrop."

Mia let out a sigh of relief. "What, then? Is something troubling you?"

Mauro paused before responding. "I've walked these streets many times, too many to count, and over the years I've had many people accompany me. First, my grandfather, then my wife, Susan, and now—"

"Me," Mia interjected. "I know you'd much rather be with your wife, and I would never even try to fill her shoes."

"It's not that," he said. "I just miss her, that's all."

Mia touched his hand. "I'm so sorry for what you're going through. I wish I knew your wife. Maybe one day when she comes home, I'll get a chance to spend some time with her."

"I hope so," Mauro replied. "She'd like you. I know she would."

Mia smiled. "What's she like?" she asked. "Tell me about her. I'd like to know."

"She's fierce but very kind. I love that about her. That juxtaposition. She can be absolutely terrifying, but so tender and loving, all in the same breath. Back in the beginning, Susan was as invested in the casket as I was, and she helped out with the investigation enormously. Without her, I wouldn't have made half as much progress as I've managed to document in my journal."

"You said 'back in the beginning,'" Mia said. "So her enthusiasm waned after a while?"

"I prefer to say we hit a brick wall," he replied. "Both of us. I'd tried many different avenues, paying investigators and experts to do some of the research for me, but all this came at a cost, and Susan didn't like how much money we were spending. Eventually, after months and months, and many thousands of dollars, she asked me to stop and refused to pay any more. You have no idea how much that hurt me."

"That she asked you to stop, or that she cut the funding?" Mia asked.

"Unfortunately, the two things were inseparable. Without money, I couldn't keep the investigation going, and without the investigation—"

"The brick wall," Mia said.

"Exactly." Mauro's breathing started to become hoarse and exaggerated as he became more and more worked up by the memory. "You see, Mia, when you believe in something as much as I believe in the mystery of the casket, you would do anything to uncover the truth. *Anything*. My wife didn't see that. She couldn't. It was as if she had become blind to it, like a mole scurrying around in the dirt."

"But the money," Mia replied. "Surely you can't just spend and spend until there's nothing left."

"The money is immaterial!" he exclaimed, slamming his hand on the bench. "If only we had kept up the momentum. If only Susan hadn't been so goddamn stubborn."

"It's okay," Mia replied, resting her hand on his arm. "It's okay. Please don't become agitated. I worry about your heart."

"My heart is fine," he hissed. "And it will be better still once we get to the bottom of this."

"But how?" Mia asked. "If the Archives don't contain any clues about what really happened, what more can we do?"

"We break in," he said in a whisper. "We sneak into the basilica, and we open the casket. It's the only way to know for sure."

"We break into the Basilica of Santa Maria Gloriosa dei Frari? Are you serious?"

"I've never been more serious about anything in my life."

Mia watched the older man for signs that this was all just a joke, but his face remained impassive, his eyes steely. He meant what he said, he really did. He truly believed that breaking into a medieval church was a reasonable thing to do.

"Okay," she said. "Maybe we can talk about this some more later, but right now, I'm so warm. I suggest we head back to the hotel, take advantage of the air conditioning in our rooms, and think about what to do next."

"I know what to do next," Mauro said, leaping up from the bench as if spilling out his plan had relieved him of the anxiety that had been crippling him. "All we have to do is figure out how."

Mia sat there for a moment and watched the older man walk along the canal. He was a riddle, a puzzle she needed to solve, and right at that very moment, the thought excited her more than anything she had ever researched at college. Whatever the risks, she planned to see this through, even if it meant going against the wishes of the love of her life.

They sat on the balcony overlooking the river and watched as the boats sailed past. Mia was sipping a cup of tea, while Costanza sat beside her, sucking on a cigarette and letting the smoke out through her nostrils.

"That's the third cigarette you've had in the past ten minutes," Mia said. "Are you sure you're okay?"

"If I'm anxious, it's because of you," Costanza replied.

"Because of me? And what have I done to cause it?"

"I am concerned for you. I'm worried about what my uncle will make you do."

"Costanza, I'm an adult woman with my own mind. Nobody makes me do anything I don't want to do."

"And yet you would listen to my zio asking you to break into a church with him. It's madness."

"I never said I would do it."

"He's just had a heart attack!" Costanza cried, blowing more smoke. "He's flown all this way on some hairbrained scheme, and now he thinks he's recruited a conspirator to his insanity."

"As I said, I never agreed to anything."

Costanza jabbed the hand holding her cigarette at her. "But you're thinking about it."

"You have to understand your uncle," Mia replied. "This whole thing with the casket, it started off with his grandfather, but then it became a thing between him and your aunt Susan. It's such a personal mission. I think he really needs this right now, especially with Susan still missing. I think it's connecting him to her in some way, as if chasing down this mystery is bringing him closer to the woman he loves."

Costanza grimaced. "You're always such a romantic. Isn't it possible that this isn't about Susan at all? It's just an obsession my zio has been carrying with him ever since he was given that journal."

"Maybe," Mia replied. "But I don't think so."

"I don't trust him, and right now, I don't trust you."

Her fiancée's words cut Mia to the core. "What's that supposed to mean?"

"It means that you've become so besotted by this, you'll do anything to see it through."

"I wouldn't."

"You would."

"No, Costanza," Mia replied, getting up from her seat. "I said I wouldn't, and I mean it."

Costanza ashed her cigarette. "And so, you're telling me you won't break into that church."

Mia folded her arms, the anger burning in her belly like a smoldering candle as she glared at her partner. She wanted to tell Costanza that she could do what the hell she liked, and if that meant breaking into a basilica and rummaging through the remains of a man who had been dead for half a century, then that was what she was going to do, but deep down she knew she couldn't say that, because to do so would threaten the one thing she cherished most in the world: the relationship she shared with this gorgeous, highly intelligent woman with an ass to die for.

"I won't," she said through gritted teeth. "I promise. I'll talk him out of it."

As night descended on the city, a train rolled into the station, and a few weary passengers stepped out from its sleepy confines, bags clutched within tired arms, eyes heavy, bellies hungry.

Inspector Wallace was the first to emerge onto the station's steps and look around for a cab. With none in sight, he headed to the water where a boatman stood, tying his vessel to the cleats.

"You guys have Uber around here?" he asked, half-peering at his phone.

"Uber? What is Uber?" the boatman asked.

"Never mind," Wallace replied. "Cabs? You have cabs, right?"

"Only water taxis."

"You mean I have to get on a boat?"

"If you want to travel fast. There are other slower means, of course."

"Which are?"

The boatman pointed to the inspector's brogues. "In the absence of horses, the road to a man's bed is best served by his feet."

"What is that? A line from a movie?"

"I read it somewhere," the boatman replied. "Now, do you want a water taxi, or will you exercise those long legs of yours?"

Wallace shook his head and turned away, no longer in the mood for this discussion. He was hungry and thirsty, and if that meant he had to walk the streets of Venice at night while dragging his stupid suitcase behind him, then that's what he was going to do. Nothing would prevent him from getting to the bottom of the Susan Imperi mystery before he retired, not even a strange Italian guy with a boat and a head full of riddles.

CHAPTER THIRTEEN

MILAN – 1990

Mauro and Susan stood in the cemetery, watching as the many funeralgoers stood by the open grave, the casket placed on the bier beside it. Mauro hadn't seen it coming. His father had always been so strong. He would never have expected this stoic bull of a man to take his own life. He was a Catholic, and in the Catholic faith, suicide was considered a sin. Hadn't it been his father who had bestowed the virtues of his faith in his young son? Hadn't it been his father who had steered a young Mauro away from the historical fancies of his grandfather and guided him to the wise words of a priest?

"Are you okay?" his wife asked. "Would you like me to give you a moment?"

"No, I'm fine," Mauro replied. "The quicker this is over, the better."

The priest read out a section of the Bible, followed by a beautiful eulogy written by his younger sister, and slowly but surely, the casket was lowered into the ground. As it disappeared from view, Mauro felt his stomach turn. This was his dad, the man who had raised him—a man who, despite his flaws, had taught Mauro how to ride a bike, swim, and shoot a gun. What would he do without him? Who would he go to for advice now that he was no longer at home, sitting in his chair, complaining about his various illnesses—the same illnesses that had driven him to take his own life?

"I'll miss him," Federica said, the tears flowing down her cheeks.

"I'll miss him, too."

"I can't believe it's come to this," she added. "If I'd have known, I would have—"

"There was nothing any of us could have done. This wasn't about us. He was suffering, and he wanted it to end."

"But, like this?"

"He just wanted a way out, Federica. It didn't matter how."

She broke down then, arms crossed over her body as her shoulders shuddered and her chest heaved. Mauro and Susan wrapped their arms around her, and the three of them stood together, consumed by their shared grief, knowing this moment would forever be etched into their memories.

A gathering was held at Federica's apartment in Milan, where some of the guests came back to pay their respects. Some stood on the balcony, others in the living room, glasses in hand.

"I still can't wrap my head around what happened," Federica said as she topped up Susan's glass. "It just doesn't make sense to me."

"You know, if my body was deteriorating like that, I might have done the same thing," Susan replied. "It can't have been easy having to live with so many disabilities."

"His actions were nothing less than cowardly," Federica spat. "He didn't think about those he would leave behind, the people that cared for him, who loved him."

Susan rubbed Federica's back, attempting to soothe away her pain.

"Please, Mauro," Federica said, her words slurring a little from the wine. "Please don't go back to Houston straight away. I've missed you, we all have. Can't you spend some more time with your family here in Milan?"

"We've spoken about this already," Mauro said. "Susan and I are really busy with work. We need to get back as soon as possible."

"But Mauro, please," Federica said. "Just a few more days."

"I'm sorry, but we can't," Mauro replied, eyeing his wife. "If we could, we would. You know that."

Federica turned her head away, hiding her tears. "Well, if you must go," she said, "I have something I need to give you."

She disappeared into the bedroom, closing the door behind her. Mauro glanced at Susan and rolled his eyes.

"You shouldn't mock her like that," Susan said. "She cares for you. That's not a bad thing."

"You're right," Mauro said. "Of course you are."

When Federica returned, she was carrying an old journal, yellow pages bound with leather.

"He wanted me to give you this," she said.

"Who?" Mauro replied, taking the book.

"Who else? Our father."

Mauro looked at it. There was a note written in Italian on the front, the hurried scrawl matching his father's own hand.

Nonno was right, it said. *Solve this at whatever cost.*

"What is this?" Mauro asked. "Some sort of diary?"

"Of sorts," Federica replied. "It was that old obsession of grandfather's. I think dear old Dad became quite taken with it in the end."

"You mean the black casket?" Mauro asked, remembering his father complaining to his nonno about revealing too much to his son. "Dad never liked to talk about it."

"People change, Mauro. Times change. Perhaps in his final days, Dad wanted to be close to his father, and this was his way of doing it. Maybe, by giving it to you now, he's trying to show how much he loved you."

Mauro looked down at the book, wondering what secrets lay inside, and whether the answers that had eluded his grandfather would now be revealed for the whole world to see.

"This is really quite interesting," Susan said, flicking through the journal while sipping the glass of Sauvignon the business-class flight attendant had handed to her. "Did you know your father was researching an old Venetian artifact?"

Mauro nodded. He'd already read some of what was written inside, and the words and images had brought back a whole headful of memories.

"I think your grandfather researched it first," she continued, munching on a crisp bread. "Because the writing is different on some of the pages. It looks much older, too."

"He took me to Venice," Mauro said. "My nonno, when I was much younger. He made us visit this great big church with beautiful paintings and intricate sculptures. I was captivated by it, even then. I'd never seen a room so big before. The architecture just blew me away."

"Why did he take you there?" Susan asked.

Mauro sipped his Rioja. "There was this casket."

"A black casket?" Susan asked. "He writes about that a lot."

"That's right. Anyway, this casket was attached to the wall above a door. It was the strangest thing. My grandfather couldn't stop looking at it, as if it had some sort of magical hold over him."

"Perhaps it did. It certainly implies that in the journal."

"He was obsessed with it until he died," Mauro replied. "And now it seems my father became obsessed with it, too."

"It's kind of fun though, isn't it?" Susan asked. "I mean, we both like history, and it seems that so did your father and grandfather. Maybe we can do what the note asks and get to the bottom of this."

"At whatever cost?" Mauro asked. "You really want to take it that far?"

"Well, maybe not, but it wouldn't hurt to do a little digging."

Mauro remembered his grandmother's words, the way she had begged him to solve the mystery to honor his nonno's memory. Somewhere along the way, he'd allowed that promise to be forgotten, and he'd lost sight of what really mattered. If this had been important to the two most influential men in his life, then maybe it should be important to him, too.

"Okay," he said, setting down his glass and leaning into his wife. "If you want to do this, then I want to do it, too."

"Perfect!" Susan exclaimed. "Then let's see what your father was up to these past few months."

CHAPTER FOURTEEN

MILAN - 1414

Francesco Carmagnola's palace was as impressive as it was opulent. It was a two-story construction with a brilliant white stone facade with a surrounding wall, a spacious courtyard, and a garden filled with grapevines and tall cypress trees. On the ground level, a delicate colonnade opened to the sky, welcoming air and light into the many rooms inside the luxurious building.

The palace occupied a large plot in the center of the city, quite near to the Broletto, the center of commerce, with its bustling markets and jovial street entertainers. Nearby, the new cathedral was in the process of being constructed, with every builder from the city employed by the complex project. It was expected to be the most remarkable cathedral in the whole of the region, or so the duke proclaimed, and the work was in part being funded by the many battles Carmagnola had won in the duke's name.

In the master bedroom of the great palace, Carmagnola looked out across the city. Behind him, his wife, Antonia, lay sleeping, as beautiful now as the day they'd first met. He couldn't believe all this was his. This building, his position in the duke's army, the wealth and fame bestowed upon him. If only his father could see him now.

"What's troubling you, my love?" Antonia asked, having just woken, her breasts barely covered by the silk sheets.

He looked down at her and smiled. She was everything to him: the sun, the moon, the mountains, the stars. She pulled the sheets around herself and walked to him, her third trimester belly visible through the fabric of the bed covers. She embraced him, kissing him tenderly on the cheek. She smelled of cinnamon and honey.

"Care to share your thoughts?" she said.

"It's nothing," he replied. "I'm just being sentimental."

"Sentimental? You?" she cried, smiling. "The great Carmagnola? The man who has laid waste to every opposing army in Northern Italy? Surely not that man."

"Yes, I'm afraid so," he replied. "I was just thinking about working on the farm with my father, breaking my back under the hot sun, day after day. Yet here I am, living in a luxurious palace, commanding an impressive army, with as much gold as we can spend, and to top it all off, I'm now a nobleman."

"The Count of Castelnuovo di Scrivia."

"Precisely, and I don't even know where Castelnuovo di Scrivia is."

"Neither do I, my love." Antonia smiled. "Neither do I."

They both laughed and embraced, Carmagnola's hand on his wife's swollen stomach.

"I thought I was being summoned to discuss the next military campaign," Carmagnola said. "I had no idea I would be given a noble title."

"You deserve it, my darling," Antonia replied. "For what you've done for the Visconti family, you deserve that and so much more."

Carmagnola shook his head, looking down at the baby in his wife's belly. "All I need is for our new child to be safe and well."

"And he or she will be," Antonia replied. "But you can't hide from what you are. They're saying you are now one of the most important men in Milan, second only to the duke himself."

"Maybe that's why they gave me this new title," he said. "To appease me."

"They don't know you," she replied, running a hand over his chest. "Only I can appease you, my love, and I know exactly how."

She leaned toward him and kissed him passionately, their lips touching, tongues searching.

"We will have to relocate if I am to be this count," he whispered in her ear. "Will you be okay with that?"

"If it is with you, my darling," she replied. "Then my life will remain forever complete."

As they embraced, their bodies entwined, there came a loud knock at the door.

"We're busy in here," Carmagnola yelled. "Whatever it is, it can wait."

"It's the duke, my lord," his guardsman replied.

"What of him?"

"He requests that you visit him."

"What, now?" Carmagnola asked, rolling his eyes.

"Yes, my lord. He says the matter is urgent."

Carmagnola shook his head and kissed his wife's forehead. "We'll pick up where we left off when I return," he said. "Don't forget me when I'm gone."

"I could never forget you, my darling," Antonia replied, letting the sheets fall from her body. "The question is, could you ever forget me?"

Carmagnola walked along the corridor to the duke's study, a guard at his side. He had no idea what Visconti wanted with him at this late hour, but there was one thing he'd learned when dealing with the impetuous nobleman, and that was to come running as soon as he was summoned. Filippo Maria was not known for either his patience or his good humor.

"The Count of Castelnuovo di Scrivia, my lord," the guard said as he opened the heavy wooden doors.

Carmagnola stepped inside and took in the splendor of the duke's study. It was paneled in elegant mahogany, while the bookcases contained many historical and religious texts. A painting of Filippo Maria dressed in military uniform hung from the far wall.

"Ah, that's right," the Duke said, standing and offering his hand. "I'd forgotten we'd given you that ridiculous title, Carmagnola. How does it sit with you?"

"Very well," Carmagnola replied. "It is a great honor to be afforded such a privilege."

"Nobility is hardly a privilege, believe me," the duke countered. "It comes with many hardships and more responsibilities than one man can handle on his own. You'll learn this, Carmagnola, and if you're smart, you'll figure out ways to delegate."

"I thank you for the advice, my lord. I'll certainly bear it in mind."

Carmagnola eyed the attractive woman reclining on a chaise longue beside the duke. She was dressed in a velvet dress and long pearl necklace, while her dark hair was grouped behind her head with silken strands tumbling over her slight shoulders. She had a smirk on her rouge lips, and a knowing look in her topaz eyes.

"My apologies!" the duke exclaimed, noticing the way Carmagnola looked at his female companion. "Carmagnola, may I introduce you to Lady Agnese del Maino."

"It's a pleasure to meet you," Carmagnola said, kissing the lady's hand.

"And I you," she replied. "Filippo has told me so much about you."

"All of it good, I hope."

"Most of it," she smirked. "I hear you have had a great many military exploits."

"It is true that God has looked favorably upon my army," Carmagnola said.

"Nonsense!" the duke cried. "You are quite a brilliant commander, and your men do as you ask. God has nothing to do with it."

Carmagnola bowed his head. "I thank you for your kind words, my lord."

"Kind words are earned, my friend, and you have done much to earn my favor." The duke glanced at Lady Agnese, who was watching his every move. "Which is why I asked you to visit with me this evening. I have a little... problem... I need your help with."

"Anything, my lord," Carmagnola replied. "You have my allegiance, I swear to it."

"Very good, very good. Well, you see, Agnese and I love each other very much, and we'd like to spend more time together. In fact, we've spoken about it at length, and we would very much like to marry." The duke unconsciously played with the wedding ring on his finger.

"Have you considered your current wife?" Carmagnola replied.

"I have indeed."

"And this is the problem of which you speak?"

"It is," the duke said. "You see, that particular alliance has reached what I like to think of as a natural conclusion, but my wife doesn't agree. In fact, she is quite taken with me, to the point of being unwilling to come to some sort of compromise."

"I see," Carmagnola said.

"Yes, it is a problem. Personally, I think she's being quite unreasonable, but she really can be quite pig-headed when the mood takes her."

"She's a nasty piece of work," Agnese spat.

"I perhaps wouldn't put it as candidly as the good lady," the duke said. "But I do have sympathy with her view."

"So... you want me to see what I can do?" Carmagnola asked.

"I do," the duke replied. "But... be discreet. You accomplish every mission I give to you with such excellence, and I would expect no less of this particular... endeavor."

"As you wish, my lord," Carmagnola replied, knowing exactly what his master was asking of him, and also knowing it was a much darker affair than anything he'd ever been requested to do before.

"See, Agnese," the duke said, planting a kiss on the lady's mouth. "I told you the count would get where I'm coming from. We have a good relationship, he and I, do we not, Carmagnola?"

"Indeed we do."

"And so you'll deal with this... problem... of mine, and keep me out of it."

"You don't need to worry yourself, sir," Carmagnola said, knowing this was the response the duke wanted to hear. "The deed will be done, and nobody will point the finger of blame in your direction."

The duke thrust into his lady, his hips pounding against her bared buttocks faster and faster until the exaltation of his exquisite climax rippled through his body. He collapsed on the bed beside her, breathless and covered in sweat. The lady lay in his arms, her hand stroking his chest and abdomen, her lips kissing his neck and shoulder.

"I told you he would do it," he whispered to her. "Although, I must confess, I hadn't expected him to convince the courts of some fictitious adultery."

"Whatever he did, it worked," Agnese replied. "I watched the execution myself. The look on her grotesque face was priceless."

"I wish I could have been there," the duke said. "But I fear, if I had traveled to the gallows, the whole of Northern Italy would have been talking."

"Trust me when I tell you it was a glorious event, my love," Agnese said. "And now we can do what we have wanted for so long. We can be married."

The duke propped himself on one elbow and kissed her passionately. "Let's do it this month," he said.

"This month? But—"

"No buts, my darling. We have wasted too much time already because of that horrid woman. Now that the way ahead is clear, we can do whatever we want."

"Not quite," Agnese said, sitting upright and pulling her robes across her body.

"What do you mean?" the duke asked.

"I mean, the way ahead is not quite clear."

"In what way, my love?"

"That man, Carmagnola—you have given him too much power."

"Too much power? He commands my army. The man needs power in order to do my bidding."

"You have given him something he can use against you," Agnese replied. "What is to stop him from telling anybody who will listen that you were the one who requested he frame that evil woman?"

"He wouldn't," the duke said. "We're friends."

"Are you? Are you sure about that? This man has already shown himself to be a ruthless mercenary. Are you seriously telling me he wouldn't do whatever it takes to secure the kind of wealth and power you possess?"

"You think he means to seize control of the city?"

"I think if he wants to, he now has the means to do so."

The duke turned away from her. He hadn't even considered the possibility that Carmagnola could turn against him. He always seemed too happy to please, so willing to do his bidding. But now that he thought about it, there was often that mischievous glint in his eye, and sometimes the duke would catch him whispering in the corridors.

"You have to do something," Agnese said. "If we are truly to be wed, you have to deal with the count."

Carmagnola sat around the table with his lieutenant, Bernardo, reviewing the maps and plans of Brescia, the next city they had been ordered to seize. He was growing tired of the endless battles and ceaseless warfare, but the duke wanted to press home their advantage, and there was no better way of doing that than securing a stronghold to the east of Milan.

"So we approach from the south," Carmagnola said. "We storm the gates while sending a platoon on horseback to attack from the east. I know Brescia well, and they do not have the defenses to withstand a two-pronged assault."

Bernardo leaned over the table, drawing lines across the landscape and marking where every one of their battalions would be stationed.

As the candlelight flickered, there was a noise from outside, the sound of men shouting and swords clashing. Bernardo headed for the window.

"There are Ducal soldiers, my lord. They're storming the palace."

Carmagnola rushed to him. He peered out into the darkness and saw three soldiers attacking his guards, and a dozen more soldiers arriving behind them.

"They're the duke's men," he said, recalling the task he'd carried out for his master, and the fear that one day, that one terrible act would come back to bite him. "We need to leave."

"Go fetch your lady," Bernardo replied. "I'll hold them off."

"No, I won't leave you," Carmagnola said.

"If you don't, your wife and unborn child will be killed. Now go!"

Carmagnola headed to his wife's chambers. Antonia was standing in the doorway, her face a mask of fear.

"What is it, my love?"

"The duke has betrayed us," he replied. "We need to leave. Now!"

He placed a hand on her belly and kissed her. "Where will we go?" she asked.

"To Venice," he replied. "I have allies there."

He grabbed a leather bag from beside the bed and ushered Antonia to the kitchen. Once there, he helped her climb onto the roof, and together they clambered down the trellis toward the waiting horses. Above them, there came the sound of fierce fighting, and the call of Bernardo's voice as he drove back the attackers.

Carmagnola helped his wife up onto her steed and then climbed onto his own. As they rode off into the night, the air was filled with fierce cries and the bloody sound of murder.

Carmagnola did indeed find allies in Venice, and wasted no time in convincing the Council of Ten of his military attributes. Pretty soon, he was placed in charge of the Venetian army, and he led his men into dozens of fierce battles where he once more emerged victorious. His fame spread throughout the city and across the region. This soldier from Milan had done what no other man could. He had turned the once-mocked Venetian military into a power to be reckoned with.

While the Council of Ten celebrated their new recruit, Secretary de Imperiis was less than impressed. He had known of Carmagnola when he had been a mere trainee soldier under Facino Cane. He had watched him rise to power in Milan, and was hardly surprised when the duke had taken it upon himself to chase him from the city. Now Venice was infected with the pestilence that was Francesco Carmagnola, and if they didn't act swiftly, one day the infection would spread to every corner of the republic. The secretary folded his hands on his desk and considered his options. Something had to be done. Something that could not be undone.

CHAPTER FIFTEEN

VENICE – PRESENT DAY / MILAN – 1432

Mia walked beside her fiancée and her uncle, taking in yet more sights of the historic city. They were heading toward the basilica after Mauro had convinced them he wanted one final look at the casket. While Costanza had been reluctant, Mia had insisted. It was only fair, after all, that they bend to the wishes of the man who had so generously paid for their trip.

"So, Carmagnola was loyal to the Venetians!" she exclaimed. "I didn't see that coming."

"I suspect neither did he," Mauro replied. "You see, when a man becomes as powerful as Carmagnola eventually became, he attracts many enemies."

"But he had done everything for the Duke of Milan," Mia said. "He even framed his wife."

"And that was to be his undoing," Mauro replied. "An act as devious as that can never go unpunished, but in this instance, the man who was pulling the strings decided he needed to cut all ties in the most violent way possible."

Mia considered the events leading up to Carmagnola's flight from Milan. He'd had it so good, and yet he couldn't hold onto the life he'd built for himself and his wife. She couldn't imagine being there that night when the duke's soldiers had stormed the palace. How would she have reacted in the same situation? Would she have panicked? Would she have had the fortitude to escape when everything was so chaotic?

"So what happened in Venice?" she asked. "If Carmagnola was such a great commander, why did the Council of Ten turn against him?"

"Mia, you are so full of questions!" Costanza exclaimed. "These things happened so long ago. Why do you even care?"

"Because she is an intellectual," Mauro snapped at his niece. "And because she has an inquisitive nature. You could learn a lot from your fiancée."

"I just find the whole thing boring," Costanza replied, folding her arms and turning her head away.

"If you want to know what happened, Mia, I'll tell you," Mauro said.

Mia nodded enthusiastically. "I do. I really do."

Mauro dabbed his forehead and neck with a handkerchief and continued. "Well, you see, it is true that Carmagnola won a great many victories for Venice, and the members of the council were delighted with his progress. They could never have imagined in their wildest dreams that a man of his strength and tactical skills could ever come to lead their army, but there was one task he failed to do, and unfortunately for him, it was the most important task of all."

"Which was?" Mia asked, her brow creased.

"As with all great stories, there is always one moment where the protagonist and antagonist come face to face. In this case, our hero is Carmagnola, and our villain is Filippo Maria."

"The duke!" Mia exclaimed.

"Precisely," Mauro replied. "You see, there was no way Carmagnola's army could avoid coming into contact with the Milanese forces. When it did, a raging battle ensued, and sure enough, Carmagnola's ferocious army pushed the army of Milan back, leaving behind several hundred prisoners. The Council of Ten could feel Milan was in their grasp, but in the moment where they expected their forces to strike the fatal blow, Carmagnola pulled back, seemingly unwilling or unable to punish his old master."

"So he refused to advance?"

Mauro nodded. "Nobody knows why, not even to this day, but it was this decision that many believe ultimately led to his downfall."

"Sounds like a crazy reason," Costanza chimed in. "Just because he didn't want to kill a whole bunch of innocent people. What's wrong with that?"

"Because it made the council question his loyalty," Mauro replied. "And back then, loyalty mattered more than money or influence. It was the one thing that stood a person apart from his peers. If you were loyal to your city, your city was loyal to you."

"But if you weren't?" Costanza asked.

Mauro's expression became grave. "For that, we have to consider what happened to the count next."

Antonia stood in her chambers, brushing her long hair in front of the tall mirror as the late evening sun shone through the open window. Her daughters ran into the room, laughing and giggling as they jostled with each other.

"Darlings," she said. "Do you have to make such a noise?"

"Antonietta is chasing me, Mommy!" Luchina cried. "But I'm too fast for her."

"I'll get you," Antonietta said, her voice filled with laughter. "You can't get away from me."

"Madam," her lady in waiting said as she appeared in the doorway. "There is a visitor for you."

"A visitor?" Antonia asked. "Who would arrive at this late hour when I'm about to get my daughters ready for bed?"

"I'm afraid that would be me," Secretary Iovanni De Imperiis said, standing behind the lady in waiting. "I hope I am not intruding."

"Of course not," Antonia replied, a little perplexed. "Although it is a little late—I am sure one of my staff will be all too happy to put my children to bed."

"Oh, Mama, our story!" the girls cried.

"There will be plenty of time for stories tomorrow night," Antonia replied, eying the secretary as he entered the room. "For now, Signore Imperiis and I need to talk."

"Come on, children," the lady in waiting said, ushering the two girls to the door. "Your mother has important business to attend to."

"Thank you for seeing me," Imperiis said. "I know my visit is a little inopportune."

"Nonsense," Antonia replied. "You'll always be welcome in our home, Secretary, as would any other member of the council."

"You're very kind," Imperiis said.

"Would you like something to drink?" Antonia asked.

"A little wine would not go amiss," Imperiis replied. "But only if you are able to spare it."

Antonia poured him a glass. "We have plenty to spare, Secretary, and I can assure you, it is of the finest quality."

"Indeed it is," Imperiis replied, sipping from the crystal glass. "I have been traveling many hours, and I am very thirsty."

Antonia ushered him to sit. "You must be exhausted. Please, rest yourself."

Imperiis lounged on a cushioned armchair and folded his legs. "Maybe this is a good time to let you know why I'm here."

"I have been wondering that very thing," Antonia replied. "Has something happened that my husband needs to be aware of? If so, I would need to send word to him."

"No need to send word," Imperiis said. "In fact, I'm heading to Brescia to meet with him myself straight after this. The doge and I plan to discuss our new military strategy with him."

"He will be very pleased to see you," Antonia said. "But I must confess, if you're on the way to talk with him directly, what reason could you have for coming to see me?"

The secretary's gaze shifted ever so slightly as he set down his glass. After a moment, he stood and walked to the window. "There's a lot of pressure on your husband these days," he said. "So much pressure. It must be very difficult for him."

"Francesco is a strong man of both body and mind. I am very sure he can handle anything the world throws at him."

"But still, it must take its toll. Even the most hardy of soldiers would not be impervious to such a burden."

"Maybe, maybe not, but I can assure you my husband does not show it in any way."

Imperiis turned to face her, a wry smile on his lips. "Lombardy was... unfortunate," he said. "Much has been made of it. I for one am sympathetic, what with your husband's ties to the Duke of Milan."

"Ties?" Antonia exclaimed. "Perhaps you did not hear, Secretary. The duke had us chased from our home. If we hadn't acted swiftly, I am very sure he would have had us executed."

"And yet Francesco refused to crush him when he had the chance."

Antonia steeled herself, the anger bubbling in her gut like boiling water. "Are you questioning my husband's loyalty to his beloved city?"

"I am merely stating a fact."

"With a hint of malice."

"No malice intended, my lady, but even you must admit, his actions were... a little unusual."

Antonia set down her glass and walked toward the secretary, her anger now so fierce, she could barely contain it. "Watch your mouth, Secretary. You seem to be forgetting, my husband is a very powerful man."

"Perhaps not as powerful as he thinks," Imperiis replied, his gaze unwavering.

"And what is that supposed to mean?"

"The council members are not happy, Antonia. Of that, you can be in no doubt."

"And what is the impact of such... rancor?"

The secretary reached out and brushed a lock of hair from her brow, his fingers like ice against her skin. "You don't need to worry about them," he said. "I can protect you and your girls."

"And my husband?"

The secretary shook his head. "I'm afraid what happens to your husband is a matter for those who have far more authority than I."

"Then I have no need to speak with you," she replied.

"Don't be like that, dearest Antonia," Imperiis said in a voice so soft she could barely hear him. He leaned forward, his hands resting on her shoulders. "We could be a powerful partnership you and I, if only you would—"

He leaned toward her, lips pursed, hands searching her neckline.

"Secretary, what are you doing?" she exclaimed, pulling herself away.

"Just as I said," he replied, standing aghast. "If you ally yourself to your husband, I'm afraid there will be nothing I can do for you."

"Better that than to betray him!" she cried. "Now, I'm afraid I must ask you to leave."

"Very well," he hissed. "But know this: a sea of change is coming, and if you don't batten down the hatches, you will be swept out to sea."

As he departed, Antonia stood in his wake, knowing she had to get a message to her husband as soon as possible.

Carmagnola arrived home a few days later, fresh from his time in Brescia where he and his generals had made good progress. Things were looking very positive for him and his family with the power he'd managed to attain gradually growing, as were the coffers of his treasury.

"My love," he said as he entered his wife's chambers.

"You're home," Antonia replied, racing across the room toward him, throwing her arms around his neck and kissing him tenderly. "I've missed you so much."

"And I you, my darling. How have the girls been?"

"They have missed you, too," she said.

"Then fetch them," he replied. "I long to see their beautiful eyes and smiling faces."

Antonia turned from him.

"What's the matter, my love? Is something troubling you?"

Antonia shook her head. "No, it's fine. Have you... by any chance met with Secretary Imperiis?"

"I have," Carmagnola said, looking incredulous. "But how would you know that?"

"He was here," Antonia replied. "He came to warn me."

"Warn you of what?"

Antonia shied away from him. "First, tell me what he asked of you."

Carmagnola went to her and took her hands in his. "It's good news, my darling. He came to Brescia to tell me that the doge wants to meet with me. Can you believe that?"

Antonia didn't reply, choosing instead to turn her back on him.

"I think the doge wants to reward me for my efforts in Brescia," he continued, taking an apple from a tray and biting into its soft flesh. "Things just keep getting better and better for us, my love. Think of what this means for our futures. For the futures of our two beautiful girls."

"Don't go!" Antonia exclaimed. "Please, my darling, don't go to this meeting."

Carmagnola couldn't believe his ears. What was making his wife behave this way? "Refuse a meeting with the doge? Why would I want to do that?"

"Because his intentions are not sincere!" she cried. "Because he doesn't want to reward you."

"Nonsense!" Carmagnola exclaimed. "The doge has never been anything but good to us. My darling, why would you say such things?"

"Because I have a very bad feeling," she replied. "Because something in my stomach is telling me if you go to the palace, you might never return."

Carmagnola went to her and held her in his arms. To his surprise, his wife buried her face in his chest and sobbed. "What's causing this, Antonia? Why does the mention of this meeting cause you such heartache? Is it because of Imperiis's visit?"

She spoke through her sobs. "It is."

"Then you need not worry. The secretary is a pathetic little man who wallows in the success of others. Whatever he said, it's meaningless. The doge would do nothing to stand against me, and he would never heed the words of a sniveling little wretch like Imperiis."

Antonia eyed him from within his arms. "Don't go, my love," she said. "Please."

"I have to," Carmagnola replied. "But don't worry. I will be back home before you know it, with treasures you and the girls could only ever dream of."

CHAPTER SIXTEEN

VENICE – PRESENT DAY

The trio entered the basilica, which provided them shelter from the blazing hot sun.

"Did he ever make it back?" Mia asked. "Carmagnola, I mean. Please, tell me he made it home to his wife."

"I'm afraid not," Mauro replied. "It was as Imperiis suggested. The doge really was unhappy with what he saw as Carmagnola's betrayal, and he ordered him to be arrested as soon as he set foot in the palace."

"Oh God!" Mia exclaimed.

"Oh God indeed," Mauro replied, eyeing the inside of the basilica. "As the story goes, Carmagnola was tried for treason and sentenced to death. The problem is, there is no record of the trial or the execution. Even in the corridors of truth that are the Venetian Archives, there is absolutely no mention of it."

"But that's so unusual," Mia said.

"Just like everything about the casket," Mauro replied. "There's very little that makes sense. That is why I suspect Carmagnola's remains may well be hanging above that door. What better place to hide the body of a man who was executed without much evidence of his crimes than right here in the Basilica of Santa Maria Gloriosa dei Frari?"

Mia stared at the door at the back of the room and the black casket that hung just above the opening.

"But what about Francesco?" she asked. "Didn't he have a proper burial after the execution?"

"Why are you calling this man by his first name?" Costanza exclaimed. "The pair of you sound like you know the guy."

"I have been researching him for so long, I kind of think I do," Mauro replied.

"I feel the same," Mia said. "From your notebook, from the stories you have told me. I can't help but have sympathy for him."

"Sympathy for a man who lived more than five hundred years ago. Pff," Costanza said, turning her head. "You two sound crazy."

"But what about the funeral?" Mia asked, ignoring her. "Surely he had one."

"There wasn't a funeral or a wake," Mauro said. "Or not one that I can find a record of."

"Which is more evidence that supports your theory," Mia replied. "Why would you bury a body that is already interred?"

"Exactly!" Mauro exclaimed. "See, Costanza? She gets it, which is more than I can say about you, my own flesh and blood."

"Except there's a flaw in your theory, isn't there?" Costanza replied, her cynicism evident in her tone. "Because you once told me they opened the casket to prove once and for all who was in there."

Mia's mouth fell open. "Is that true?"

"It is," Mauro replied. "And the fact that my niece remembers that part of the story is very pleasing to me. However, it doesn't help. You see, in the nineteenth century, by order of the ruling council at that time, the casket was indeed opened, principally because the rumors of the count's remains had grown to fever pitch."

"Very interesting," Mia said. "But what was the outcome?"

"He wasn't there," Mauro replied. "Or so the records would have you believe. Instead, they found the remains of a nobleman named Alvise Della Torre who lived on the mainland in Venetian territory in the sixteenth century. Della Torre was a friend of the republic, and was killed in highly suspicious circumstances after visiting the city in an attempt to resolve a dispute."

"You mean, he was murdered, too?"

Mauro nodded. "Allegedly, he was ambushed by a rival family by the Grand Canal, and executed as retribution for prior slayings."

"But he was in the casket, right?" Costanza asked.

"The investigating officers in the nineteenth century appeared to conclude that, yes, which is why they painted the fresco behind the casket."

"The drapes with the Della Torre crest!" Mia exclaimed. "I read about that in your notebook."

"Then you will know the findings are flawed," Mauro said. "And that many believe Della Torre's remains were placed in the casket purely for the benefit of the investigating council, and that the actual remains were hidden somewhere on the premises."

"To be returned when the coast was clear," Mia said, the excitement palpable in her eyes.

"You've got to be kidding me," Costanza said. "Why can't the truth just be the truth? These people proved that Della Torre was in the casket, yet the two of you doubt what is a matter of record."

"Because of the evidence that contradicts their findings," Mauro said.

"And the mounting evidence that Carmagnola is actually the one interred in the basilica," Mia added.

"Precisely," Mauro replied. "Which is why we actually have to take a look for ourselves."

"Which is breaking the law," Costanza said. "Which means you're willing to risk your freedom for a crackpot theory neither of you have any way of substantiating."

"But in doing so, we correct history!" Mauro exclaimed. "Can't you see that, my niece? The historians have it all wrong, as do those who run this city. What excites me is the chance that we could right a terrible wrong."

"And I feel the same way," Mia replied. "Honestly, Cos. If you could just read the journal and see what I have seen..."

"Well, as you two know more than any other scholar of Venetian history that has ever lived," Costanza said, folding her arms. "Tell me, how do you plan to achieve this great unveiling of yours."

Mauro looked inside the basilica at the cherry picker that was parked nearby. As Mia took in the appearance of the mechanical contraption, a smile danced on her lips. "You really mean to use that, don't you?"

Mauro nodded. "It is exactly the type of thing we need."

"You're joking," Costanza said. "Tell me you're joking."

Mauro ushered them to a quiet corner. "We do it tonight," he said to Mia. "When the church is closed, and the streets are empty."

"Perfect," Mia replied, the excitement rattling around in her belly.

"You're mad," Costanza said. "If you think you can get away with this, Mia, you're even crazier than he is."

"Enough of your cynicism," Mauro interjected. "We're going to do this, and once and for all I will be able to prove to Susan that I was right."

"She didn't agree with what you were doing?" Mia asked, glancing at Costanza.

"We had a quarrel, it's true," Mauro said. "In fact, the last words we ever spoke were about her desire for me to stop what she considered to be nonsense. It doesn't seem like nonsense now, does it?"

As they left the basilica, Mia wondered about that. Although the thrill of the chase had her in its icy grasp, she also knew there was a chance they were wrong. What then? How would Costanza's uncle react if what they found in the casket wasn't the thing he'd been chasing ever since he was a little boy?

That evening, Mia sat in the bar with Costanza, sipping an Aperol Spritz and ruminating over the day's events. Across from them, Mauro sat by himself, apparently lost in his own thoughts, or too exhausted to continue his disagreement with his niece.

Mia played with the keys of her laptop, going over some of the older man's notes, thinking about their planned excursion that evening, and wondering if they really were on the brink of an important historic discovery.

Beside her, Costanza set down her glass a little louder than was necessary, spilling drink on the table and sending her straw tumbling.

"Everything okay?" Mia asked.

"I'm fine."

"You don't seem fine."

"I said I'm okay. Can we just leave it?"

Mia eyed the screen, now too anxious to look her fiancée in the eyes. "What's up?" she said. "And be honest this time. I can practically see the steam blowing out your ears."

"If you don't know why I'm angry, then perhaps you don't know me at all."

"You're worried about what we're planning?"

"Worried? *Worried?* That's the understatement of the century. I think you're insane. It's like you want to play at being Indiana Jones or Lara Croft or something. Can't you see how crazy that sounds? You want to break into one of the most sacred churches in the city to open a centuries-old casket and study dust. Jeez, you made better decisions at your graduation party."

"I know how mad it sounds," Mia replied. "But opportunities like this don't come along very often for me, and I just want to grab it with both hands, you know?"

"We don't need the money, Mia. We were doing fine without my zio's check."

"It's not about the money," Mia replied. "Don't you see? It was never about that. It's all about the discovery, our names on the report, proof that the friars lied and the man in that casket isn't who they say it is."

"But why, Mia?"

"Because your uncle is a convincing man. Because he has spent so long researching it and so did his father and grandfather. There has to be something in it."

Costanza leaned across the table and took her hands in hers. "And have you looked in his eyes lately? Have you seen the madness there? And what about my Aunt Susan? You heard him. Even she didn't believe his stories, and she knew much more about this than he ever will."

"Nobody is forcing you to be a part of this," Mia said more cruelly than she'd intended.

Costanza's eyes glistened with tears. "You're right. Nobody is, and I won't. I refuse. I came with you to Venice because this was supposed to be a vacation, some time away from everything, but it has proven to be anything but."

Mia took a breath, a moment to compose herself. Costanza had a point, she knew she did, but she also knew this was important.

"You're right," she said. "Everything you say is right, but I have to do this, Costanza. I know that sounds idiotic, but it's true. A part of me wants this so badly. I need something to... hold onto."

"I'm right here," Costanza replied.

"I know you are, and I love you for that."

Costanza eyed her uncle across the room. "Look," she said. "You do you. I'll stay, but I want no part of it. For all you know, that man over there is in the middle of a fever dream, and he's dragging you along for the ride."

"He's not in a fever dream," Mia replied, laughing. "He's just had one Martini too many."

"And in his state," Costanza sneered, "he shouldn't be touching a drop of alcohol. Not... one... single... drop."

Mauro sipped his second Martini, a Bombay Sapphire decorated with one olive for taste. As he finished the last of the sharp liquid, he held up his hand for a third, but to his surprise, the bartender was already standing there with one in his hand.

"It's for you," he said. "From the man in the booth."

Mauro turned around to see who the generous gentleman was, and to his surprise, his eyes landed on Inspector Wallace, the man in charge of finding his wife.

"Mr Imperi," the inspector said, standing and taking a seat beside him. "I thought it was you. What a coincidence, you and me being in the same city on this same fine evening. I hope you didn't mind me buying you another, only you seemed to be enjoying the first two so much."

"I don't mind at all," Mauro replied, sipping his Martini. "But you will have to allow me to return the compliment."

The inspector nodded his appreciation.

"I have to ask, however," Mauro said. "Why are you here?"

"It's a little pre-retirement celebration trip," Wallace replied. "I've been working cases for so long, I can't even remember the last time I took time off."

"Well, if it's history and culture you're looking for, you came to the right place."

"From what I've seen so far, I would have to agree," Wallace said. "A fascinating place." The inspector looked Mauro up and down. "I must say, the hospital must have exaggerated your condition, because you look the picture of good health."

"I feel great," Mauro replied. "Better than great. I feel fantastic."

"Three Martinis will do that to you," Wallace said. "It's something about the juniper berries, although, personally, I can't abide them."

"It's an acquired taste," Mauro replied. "One that my wife and I managed to become quite appreciative of."

"Although she's not here to enjoy it tonight."

"Quite."

The inspector sipped his beer. "It's my first time in Venice, and I must say, it really is quite the place. Do you come here often?"

"As often as I can, yes."

"And so you know your way around."

"I'm not a guide, if that's what you mean, but I do have a thorough knowledge of the city and its history."

"Then perhaps you can show me around when you're free."

"I have quite a schedule, Inspector, but I'll certainly let you know if I have time." Mauro reached into his pocket, extracted a handkerchief, and wiped perspiration from his brow.

"Are you okay, Mr. Imperi?"

"Fine, yes."

"You look a little hot and bothered."

"It's just the climate. It can be a little overbearing at times."

"That's humidity for you. I oughta know. I spent a lot of time down there in Florida in my youth, and I lost my body weight in sweat. Maybe I could use a little bit of that now," he said, slapping a hand on his bulging paunch.

Mauro shuffled anxiously in his seat. "Perhaps I should retire to bed, after all," he said, pushing his half-consumed drink to one side. "A beer for my friend, bartender," he called as he slipped ten euros across the bar. "But I'm afraid I really don't have the energy for further conversation. I hope you're not offended."

"Not offended at all," Wallace replied, his penetrative stare taking in Mauro's discomfort. "I'm sure I'll see you before I leave."

"Oh, I'm very sure of that," Mauro replied, looking to get away from his drinking companion as swiftly as possible. "Goodnight, Inspector Wallace."

"Goodnight, Mr. Imperi. I hope you sleep well."

As Wallace drank the last of Mauro's Martini, biting down on the olive as if it were a bug to be squashed, Costanza sat in silence on the opposite side of the room, taking everything in and silently wondering what her zio was hiding. She intended to find out, if it was the last thing she did. She wouldn't let Mia sacrifice herself for a cause neither of them truly understood.

Nighttime descended like a dark veil, its withering cloak draped over the city like the reaper's cowl. Mauro and Mia moved through the darkness, their own bodies wrapped in black clothing that camouflaged them among the flittering shadows. On their faces, they wore dark ski masks to hide their appearance, although Mia found it difficult to breathe through the thick material. They had bought the masks earlier that evening at the Italosport store close to San Marco—a relatively simple task that had taken them longer than they had planned. Finding ski gear in Venice, it seemed, wasn't an easy task.

Beside her, Mauro muttered to himself, as if something was agitating him. He pointed to the fence that surrounded the area of the courtyard they needed access to, and after a moment, they vaulted it, Mia landing rather more elegantly than her older companion.

"Are you okay?" she whispered, but Mauro didn't respond. He simply headed directly to the wooden door and leaned his shoulder into it, forcing it open.

Once inside, they headed to the cherry picker that had been placed more than thirty feet from the casket. Mauro urged Mia to help him push the equipment along the nave to the doorway behind the altar. She obliged, keeping watch on the shadows, her heart pounding in her chest. She had never done anything like this before, not even when she was at school and her fellow students constantly looked for ways to test the patience of her teachers. Maybe it was why she was going along with Mauro's quest, as if it was a way in which she could step outside of her usually rigid behavioral boundaries. Perhaps it was the excitement that drew her in, the risk factor—the chance that, at any moment, they could be caught, and the whole thing could come crumbling all around them.

Even though the cherry picker was heavy, and Mauro was hardly the picture of health, they made it to the doorway. Once there, Mauro reached for the cable and plugged the equipment into the wall.

"I'm going in," he said, before climbing into the metal frame, using the lever to raise the platform to the correct elevation. Mia watched from below, her excitement building.

With Mauro now the same height as the casket, he reached into his pocket and extracted a screwdriver, working it into the gap between the casket's body and the lid, which made a sound like a cat screeching.

"Shh," Mia urged him. "Somebody could hear us."

"I don't care," Mauro said, his face beaming with anticipation. "This is it, Mia. In a few moments, we will know the answer. We will know everything."

Mia grinned. He was right. This was what they had been waiting for. Pretty soon, the mystery of the black casket would be revealed, and the whole world would know the truth.

Costanza stood outside in the darkness, phone pushed to her ear as she dragged on her cigarette. She was nervous. Mia and her zio were inside. Anything could happen.

"Honestly, Mama," she said. "It's all he talks about. This damn casket. He's like a man possessed."

"Our father was the same. Our grandfather, too," her mother replied. "It's been something the men in our family have been obsessed with for decades."

"But why? What does he have to gain from proving his theory? He makes it sound like he and his son will be rewarded in some way if he reveals the secrets in that box."

Her mother sighed down the line. "Maybe he's agreed to some sort of arrangement with some backers," she said. "Or perhaps he's simply deluded. I don't know, Costanza, but whatever you do, don't allow yourself to get into trouble because of it."

"I won't, Mama," she replied. "It's just..."

"Just what, my darling?"

"It's just that it's like he's lost his mind. I mean, he doesn't need money, does he? Aunt Susan has plenty of it."

"He's just lost his wife of over twenty years, Costanza. Perhaps we can forgive him a little insanity at a moment like this."

"Right, but there's crazy, and then there's crazy. They're in there now, breaking into a church like a couple of petty thieves. I'm so worried for Mia."

"Don't worry. They'll be fine. Pretty soon, they'll be out, and Mauro will have what he came for. Then you and Mia can get on with enjoying your holiday."

Costanza exhaled, blowing smoke in a long plume. "Mama, you're sounding as crazy as they are."

Her mother laughed. "Perhaps I am," she said. "Perhaps I am."

As the call ended, Costanza pitched her cigarette and pulled another from the packet. Her anxiety had reached new levels. She needed nicotine like an alcoholic needed whiskey. She felt like she was standing on the edge of a knife, as if one wrong move would lead to her being sliced in half.

"Come on," she said, tilting her head to the flickering flame of her lighter. "Please, for both our sakes, Mia. Hurry up."

"What's in there?" Mia asked. "Mauro, I can't stand the suspense. What do you see?"

Mauro's face was lit by the meager light of the basilica, giving his skin a ghostly complexion. His eyes were narrow, brow furrowed, his face a mask of confusion.

"What is it?" she asked.

"These robes are not right," he said. "They're from the fifteenth century, not the sixteenth like the friars would have us believe. They couldn't possibly belong to Alvisa Della Torre."

"Then you were right," she whispered. "You were right all along."

"Perhaps," he replied, looking further. "There's something else," he said. "An inscription on the vest. It is faded and barely readable. All I can make out are the letters I, O, V, D, E, I, M, P."

"Iovdeimp?" Mia repeated. "What does it mean? It doesn't make sense."

"I don't know," Mauro replied, lowering the platform. "I just don't know."

"Are we done?" Mia asked, feeling the disappointment taking hold of her.

"There's nothing else in there," Mauro replied, gesturing for her to help him return the cherry picker to its original place. As they parked the equipment, Mauro turned to the doorway. "We'll talk outside where it's safe," he said. "We have some thinking to do."

As Mia followed behind, she couldn't help but wonder whether this whole thing had just been one big mistake, and whether the hunt for the truth inside the black casket had just been an old man's crusade to hide the hurt he felt at the disappearance of the woman he loved.

"May I borrow a lighter?" a figure asked from the shadows as Costanza drew on her cigarette.

"Of course," Costanza replied, trying to hide her shock as the man who had been talking to her zio at the bar appeared from the darkness.

She reached out with her lighter and lit his cigarette, watching as the man inhaled and turned, walking back the way he had come.

She crossed her arms, wondering what this man had seen and whether he knew more than he was letting on.

Beside the fence he'd just clambered over, Mauro looked on, wondering what his niece had been doing talking to the man who had followed him from Texas, the same man who was tasked with solving the disappearance of his wife.

"It's good to hear your voice," Mauro said, standing on his hotel balcony with his cell phone pressed to his ear, the events in the basilica still fresh in his mind. "I've missed you."

"I've missed you too, Dad," Ben replied. "Will you be coming home soon?"

"Soon, my son," Mauro said. "I've almost finished what I came to do here."

"What even is it you're doing?" Ben asked.

"A family thing," Mauro replied. "It was something your mother and I were looking into. I feel like I owe it to her to see it through."

"You're not in trouble, though, right?"

"No. No trouble at all," Mauro said as he laughed. "When have you ever known your old man to get himself into any difficulties?"

"I must admit, you're pretty good at dodging bullets," Ben replied, also laughing.

"I do have a question to ask you, however," Mauro said.

"Sure," Ben replied. "What is it?"

"Has... anybody come around recently, asking after me?"

"Not that I can remem—oh, wait." Ben paused. "There was the detective. He came by. He was talking about his retirement, said he wanted to tell you himself. I told him where you were staying. I hope that was okay."

Mauro's heart sank. He knew there had been something off about Wallace. He wasn't in Venice by chance, after all. He had come looking for him, and that could only mean one thing.

"You did exactly the right thing, son. Listen, I have to go, but I'll be home soon. I promise."

"Okay. I love you, Dad."

"I love you, too, son."

As the phone line disconnected, Mauro stared down at the blank screen, knowing that time was running out. He had to stay ahead of Wallace and get to the bottom of the mystery before it was too late.

Behind him, hidden by the shadows, Wallace stood on his balcony, crushing out the remains of his cigarette and smiling. He'd heard the things that Mauro had said to his son, and he'd also picked up on the anxiety in his voice. That was good. It was real good. Things were going his way at last, which meant the solution to his problem was in plain sight. Maybe, just maybe, he could retire with an empty roster and a satisfied conscience. Wouldn't that be just the cherry on the cake? A cherry from a cherry picker, perhaps.

CHAPTER SEVENTEEN

HOUSTON – TWO YEARS PRIOR

As Mauro walked into his home, he knew instantly that something was wrong. The whole place reeked of upset, as if the vibrations in the atmosphere were moving so rapidly, the whole place could collapse at any second.

He headed to the living room and saw his wife sitting on the couch, her arms folded, lips pursed into a thin welt.

"I'm home," he said, forcing a smile. "Everything okay?"

"You thought I wouldn't notice, I assume," Susan replied, her expression emotionless.

"Thought you wouldn't notice? Give me a clue, my love. What is it you're referring to?"

"You know exactly what I'm talking about," she said, holding up a sheet of paper. "My credit card statement. You've been spending money like it's going out of fashion."

"Wait, I can explain that," he said, crossing the room.

"Of course you can. You always have some excuse."

"I met with a woman, Susan. A specialist."

"I can see that," Susan hissed, looking at the bill. "Renee Walker, Leading Expert in the Occult. You paid this woman almost $8,000 of my money without even mentioning it to me."

"I had to act quickly," Mauro said. "Specialists like Renee are very busy. She had a gap in her schedule, and I decided to snap it up. If I hadn't, we could have been waiting months for another appointment to appear."

"We? *We?* You say that like I would have agreed to this."

Mauro felt his anger rising. "You told me you were okay with me researching the casket."

"Yes! Research! Not spend every damn dollar we have."

"This is important, Susan! Can't you see that? My father died because of this curse."

"What curse, Mauro? Your father didn't die because of some hex. He committed suicide because he couldn't live with his physical limitations. It happens all the time. It's sad, but that's the truth."

"Then why would my grandfather warn me?" Mauro yelled. "Why would he ask me to break the curse at all costs?"

"Stop trying to emotionally blackmail me, Mauro. You know as well as I do that this obsession has nothing to do with family, just like you paying for another woman to travel with you to Venice has nothing to do with this supposed curse."

"And what's that supposed to mean!"

"It means exactly what it sounds like. You took another woman to Venice, paid for her hotel room in the same hotel you were staying in, and then took her out for dinner. If you're going to have an affair, Mauro, at least have the intelligence to use your own card."

Mauro's mouth opened and closed as he searched for the right words. She had it all wrong, of course she did. It was true that he and Renee had spent some alone time together, but it was all in furtherance of the cause. If his emotions had gotten the better of him, that wasn't down to him. It was down to the curse. Everything was caused by this goddamn curse.

"This is a dead end, Mauro," Susan said. "The end of the line. Whatever this is, it's gotten hold of you. You're out of control, way in over your head. It has to stop."

"No," Mauro replied, a sensation of dread taking hold of him. "You have to trust me just a little longer. Just a little more money, and then—"

"And then what? You'll find some other woman to take away with you? You'll find some other reason to get your dick out of your pants? Mauro, you couldn't even be faithful to me when I was carrying Ben!"

"This was the last time, Susan. I promise. Whatever you think of me, I'm not a womanizer. I'm not that guy!"

"My credit card statement disagrees with you," she replied, waving the piece of paper as tears welled in her eyes. "You don't care about me," she said. "You never have. If I meant anything to you, anything at all, you would stop now."

"I can't!" he replied. "Can't you see that? I don't know how."

Her expression shifted from upset to stoic determination. "Then find a way," she said, standing abruptly. "Because as of this moment, your line of credit has been cut off. You're on your own, Mauro. I'll have no further part of this."

As she walked out, leaving him standing there like a fish out of water, Mauro's anger swelled in his gut. He'd make her change his mind. He had to. This couldn't end here. He had to get to the bottom of the mystery. He couldn't let his wife stand in the way of his destiny.

CHAPTER EIGHTEEN

VENICE – PRESENT DAY

Mia sat in the Venetian Archives, scanning document after document related to the casket. She couldn't stop thinking about what they'd found, the faded monogram with the letters I, O, V, D, E, I, M, and P, and the clothing from the century prior to Alvise Della Torre's murder. None of it made any sense. They were missing something, a vital clue. They had to be.

She rifled through a pile of books she had already scanned, frustrated with her lack of progress. This was what she had studied at university—the ability to find historical needles in haystacks so deep, you could easily become buried in them—but this needle was proving too elusive. She was exhausted. The events of the prior evening had drained her energy supplies even more than she had anticipated. She ran a hand through her hair, feeling like she was a failure. Mauro was paying her good money for her expertise, and yet, right at that moment, she felt like she had no skills at all.

Her thoughts were interrupted by her phone buzzing beside her, and she glanced at it to see Costanza's number glaring back at her. She answered it.

"Hi," she said. "I'm... I'm a little busy right now."

"Are you still at the archives?" Costanza asked.

"I am," Mia whispered. "It's a little difficult to talk. Is it urgent?"

"Urgent? Of course it's urgent. Have you seen the state of my zio?"

"But that's why I'm here," Mia replied. "You see, the things we found last night, they're not consistent with the story the friars gave. It can't be Alvise Della Torre in that casket. It just can't."

"Forget that now!" Costanza exclaimed. "My zio is out of control. You have to come back. He locked himself out and just threw a tantrum in the lobby... and now he's ranting about somebody having broken into his room. I went to check it, and guess what? It's completely fine, but even though I told him so, he won't shut up about it. I can't calm him down! We need to take him home, Mia. He can't stay here. This place is making him crazy."

"I know he's not well, Cos, but you have to give me more time. We're so close now. If I can just find what I'm looking for, maybe we can solve this riddle and make your uncle well again."

"We don't have any more time," Costanza replied. "If we don't get him out of Venice, I'm afraid he'll do something even more stupid."

"Just one more day," Mia pleaded, anxiously eyeing the faces that were turning in her direction. "Please, just twenty-four more hours."

There was a pause, followed by the sound of Costanza exhaling down the line. "Ma porca miseria! Fine, but just one day, not a second more. I swear, if you make me stay here with him any longer than I have to, I'll be the one going crazy."

"You're not crazy," Mia said, smiling. "You're just madly in love with me."

"Seriously, Mia. There are some strange things going on here. That guy at the bar who bought Zio Mauro a drink—he showed up at the basilica last night. I'm also pretty sure he's staying here at the hotel. I... I think he's following us."

"I think you're being paranoid," Mia replied. "Look, it's really hard to talk right now, but I can be free in around thirty minutes. Meet me for lunch near the basilica. I'll send you a location."

"But, Mia, wait—"

"Like I said, I have to go. Keep checking your phone. I'll send the location over in a little while."

"Mia, I—"

Mia hung up, just as the clerk arrived at her desk.

"Everything okay, madam?" the clerk asked.

"Yes, fine," she said.

He looked down at her phone. "We do demand silence in the Archives, so if you wouldn't mind—"

"My apologies," Mia replied, turning her phone on silent. "It won't happen again."

Mia watched the clerk depart, angry with Costanza for interrupting her flow, but also knowing that her fiancée was right. Mauro was acting increasingly irrational, and every second they remained in Venice was bound to make matters worse. She was on the clock now, a timer that was rapidly counting down to zero.

She opened one of the thicker books, a detailed history of Venice in the sixteenth century, and flicked through the pages. There had to be something in here, something that might help her piece the clues together. Perhaps they'd been looking at the wrong time period all along. She grabbed another book, this one from the fifteenth century, and thumbed through the chapters, looking for anything to do with the execution of the Count of Carmagnola. Mauro had mentioned the Council of Ten, which from her recollection was the governing body in the City of Venice for almost 500 years from the fourteenth century onward, a collection of magistrates who were appointed to stamp out any uprisings or plots against the state, including imposing punishments on nobles that stepped out of line.

After a moment, she found the list of council members at the time of Carmagnola's beheading. Her heart sank as she read the names, none of which meant anything to her, but then she saw one that stood out. The secretary himself, Iovanni De Imperiis. Something about him spoke to her, and she let out a little squeal of joy. She shrank into herself as she realized people were looking at her, and as she continued scrolling, something else leaped off the page. She jumped up immediately and collected her things. She was so excited now, she could barely contain herself.

She headed for the exit, waving to the clerk who had clearly had enough of her distractions, and descended the steps to the street, reaching for her phone as she headed in the direction of Piazza San Marco.

"Cos," she said as her partner's voicemail kicked in. "I found something interesting. It might be something, it might be nothing, but I'm pretty sure the monogram in the casket refers to this guy, and according to the records, there's a painting of him in the Palazzo Ducale. I'm heading there now. When you get this, come and meet me. I think I have it, Cos. I really think I do."

CHAPTER NINETEEN

VENICE – PRESENT DAY

Costanza was frustrated. Mia was running in circles for her uncle, doing things she shouldn't be doing, and or what? For a paycheck? For some misguided notion of historical justice? She had nothing to prove, and while the money would be nice, they could live without it.

She lit a cigarette as she walked, puffing on it furiously as she headed to the canal. A Vaporetto stood waiting for her, so she climbed on board, but just as the boat was about to depart, she noticed she had a missed call. Realizing it was from Mia, she held it to her ear, and hearing her beloved once more recounting theories about things that happened such a long time ago, she reluctantly raised a hand to the captain.

"I have to get off," she said.

"But, Signora, we are just about to—"

"I know, and I'm sorry," she replied. "But this is urgent."

She stepped off the boat onto the walkway, but just as she turned, she bumped into the man who had asked her for a light the night before.

"Pardon my clumsiness," Wallace said. "I'm so sorry. I really didn't see you."

"It's fine," she replied, feeling anxious at once more running into this guy. "Why are you following me?"

Wallace looked offended. "Following you? Why... why would I do that?"

"You tell me," Costanza said. "First at the hotel bar, then at the basilica, and now here."

The man's guard slipped, and he reached into his pocket to extract his wallet. He pulled a card from inside and handed it to her.

"Inspector Wallace," she said, reading the inscription. "Houston, Texas, Police Department."

"I'm the man charged with finding your Aunt Susan," he said. "I'm here to follow new leads, while also keeping an eye on your uncle. He really is a hard man to keep track of."

"Is he in trouble?" Costanza asked, handing the card back.

"That I can't say," Wallace replied. "Not yet, anyway. Look, I'm sorry I troubled you. I really didn't mean to bump into you like that."

"It's okay," she said, backing away. "But look, I'd really appreciate it if you'd stop following me. I'm planning on leaving with my fiancée real soon, so it's really my uncle you should be keeping watch of. He's sick, really sick. I think his heart attack has changed him somehow. It's affected his mind. So, yes, please, if you're planning on staying, please make sure he's safe."

She raced away, keen to put as much distance between herself and the strange detective as quickly as she could. She had a feeling Wallace wasn't telling her everything, which meant her uncle was hiding something, too. She just didn't know what.

Mia made it to the Palazzo Ducale and stepped inside. Her jaw dropped as she entered. The place was a mosaic of beautiful paintings, complex architecture, and ornate sculptures. It was like a vessel from another time, a piece of medieval Italy that had been frozen in place. She stood that way for a few moments before realizing she'd come here for a reason. She had to find the painting.

"Excuse me," she asked the attendant. "Can you direct me to the Sala dell'Avogaria?"

"It's that way, Signora," the man replied. "Up the stairs to the loggia floor."

She moved through the crowd as swiftly as she could, her heart in her throat as her excitement built. She was so close now, she could taste it. This was the moment all their questions would be answered. She couldn't believe she hadn't thought of it before. I, O, V, D, E, I, M, and P.

Iovanni De Imperiis.

She entered the room, which was steeped in history. She paused at the door. She could almost feel the councilors seated there, discussing orders of the day and the noblemen who deserved to feel their wrath. The walls were covered in dark wood, the floor brown marble.

She headed inside and stood in the center of the floor, scanning the walls above her, looking for the one person she needed to find. She knew he was there somewhere. She just had to take her time. There were several paintings, all depicting censors, magistrates who were tasked with helping to keep moral order. These men were ordered to ensure there was no electoral fraud and to protect the state's public institutions, but they were also close associates with the Council of Ten. Above the door was a collection of these censors surrounding a painting of Madonna col Bambino. To her left was another painting of four censors standing either side of a wounded Jesus. Both of these paintings were magnificent in their detail and religious relevance, but it was the painting to her right that interested her the most.

There were a further four censors depicted on this image, each of them dressed in red robes, but it was the man in the middle who startled her. It was the man she had read about in the Archives, but it could also have been the man she had been spending almost every waking minute with since they'd set foot in Venice. The resemblance was uncanny, the bold jawline, dark hair, inquisitive eyes, and sharp cheek bones. He even had the same build, broad across the shoulders and thick across the chest. She fumbled in her pocket for her cell phone and held it up to the painting just as a group of tourists entered the room, led by a tour guide holding up an umbrella to ensure the eager-eyed enthusiasts followed her. She focused the screen on the man in the center of the fresco before taking a shot, and then jostled to get through the small opening, the tour guide launching into an animated description of the artwork displayed on the walls above them as she hastily departed. She had to find Mauro and Costanza. She had to tell them about this. She had no idea what it meant, but it had to mean something. It was like they were on a revolving door of history, and somehow the circle was closing in on them.

Costanza raced to the palace, eager to find Mia and tell her all about the persistent detective, but as she stepped into the square, her uncle confronted her, his eyes animated and wild.

"What did you tell him?" he hollered. "What did you reveal to the inspector?"

"Zio, I—" Costanza said, looking down at her uncle's hand on her arm. "You're hurting me."

"What did you say to him? Tell me!"

"I didn't say anything. I just asked him to keep an eye on you. I'm worried about you, zio. You're not well." She pulled her arm away. "Now let go of me."

"Can't you see?" he replied. "I'm trying to protect you. I'm to protect our family! This curse, it's been following us around for hundreds of years, but I'm on the verge of destroying it for good."

"There you go again!" she cried. "You need to let this go, Uncle. You need to get back to being just you."

"I've been watching you," he said. "I've been keeping a close eye on you and that deceitful detective. You've been meeting with him in secret, telling him things about me that you shouldn't. The two of you together are plotting against me."

"Why would you think such a thing? I would never do that. What would I have to gain?"

"You want to stop me!" he hollered, drawing anxious glances from passers by. "You've been against what Mia and I have been doing from the start. It's as clear as the nose on your face. You would do anything to sabotage me!"

"That's just not true. I haven't been meeting with Wallace. It's him who has been stalking me."

"A lie!" he cried. "Just like all your other lies!"

"What's going on?" Mia asked as she approached. "Are you two quarreling again?"

"My uncle seems to think I'm some sort of undercover spy," Costanza replied, reaching for her cigarettes. "Can you believe that?"

"Well, you won't believe this," Mia said. "I found a painting in the Chamber of Censors of Iovanni De Imperiis. Look." She unlocked her cell phone and showed them the image.

"Mio Dio!" Mauro cried. "In Sala dell'Avogaria? Tell me, Mia. This was in the Chamber of Censors?"

"To the right of the door," Mia said. "I found a reference to it in the Archives. Can you believe it, Mauro? This is the man whose monogram we found in the casket."

Mauro raced toward the palace, leaving the pair of them in his wake. Mia turned to follow him, but Costanza grabbed her arm.

"Don't," she said. "Just leave him."

"But without me—"

"Without you, he'll be fine," Costanza replied. "He's going to do what he's going to do, with or without you."

"Then what do you want us to do?" Mia asked.

"Leave," Costanza said. "Now. We have to leave Venice as soon as possible."

"What? Now? Right when we're on the verge of solving this thing?"

"He just attacked me," Costanza replied. "My own uncle, all because he thinks I've been telling Inspector Wallace secrets about what he's up to."

"Inspector Wallace? Who's Inspector Wallace?"

"The head of the homicide department of Houston, Texas."

"As in Texas, USA?"

"The very same. He followed my uncle here because he thinks the casket is connected to Aunt Susan's disappearance."

"He thinks she might have come here?" Mia asked.

Costanza shook her head as she lit her cigarette, exhaling smoke in a long plume. "I don't think she left, Mia. I think she was murdered, and I think the Inspector believes that, too."

"Oh, my God."

"We have to get away, Mia. I can't be involved in this any longer. It's all getting way too real."

"But the mystery..."

"I don't care about the mystery. He attacked me!"

"I'm sure he was just worked up. Don't you see how exciting this is? We could get to the bottom of the mystery of the black casket, and we could also help solve the case of your aunt's disappearance."

Costanza looked incredulous. "Did you just hear me say that I think she was murdered?"

"I did, but I can't believe that, Costanza. I refuse to believe that's true."

"I'm... I'm out!" Costanza cried, tears welling in her eyes. "I just can't do this."

"No, please," Mia said, reaching for her. "Just hear me out."

Costanza backed away, hands raised. "I'm sorry, Mia, but I'm done with this. You go have fun playing with the dead."

Mia went to chase after her, but a crowd of enthusiastic tourists blocked her path, and by the time they'd departed, Costanza was gone.

Mia stood still, hands in her pockets, wondering what she should do or where she should go. This had all gone so horribly wrong. She wondered about the image of Iovanni De Imperiis in the palace, of the monogram in the casket, and of Mauro's wife, Susan. She tried to understand how it all fit together, and what the inspector from Houston had to do with it all. She wondered about the striking similarities between Costanza's uncle and the secretary of the Council of Ten, and whether that had any relevance to their investigation. But most of all, she wondered about her fiancée:

where she was going, what she was thinking, and did Costanza still love her?

As she stood there, pondering the choices she'd made and the decisions she might need to make, her phone rang in her pocket.

"Hello?" she said, pressing her cell phone to her ear.

"It's me," came the reply.

"Mauro?"

"One and the same," he said. "I was just wondering. Are you hungry?"

CHAPTER TWENTY

VENICE – PRESENT DAY / VENICE – 1432 / VENICE – 1549

Mia sat in the restaurant, Osteria da Fiore—which was filled with the heady scents of rich tomato sauce, succulent pasta, and delicately cooked sea food—and gazed at her phone. There were no notifications. None. She'd hoped at least for a message from Costanza to tell her she was okay, but her phone just stared back at her with a blank expression. She pushed it to one side and sipped a glass of wine. She didn't want it, but she needed something to push the memory away. Had she really screwed up the one good thing that had happened to her since leaving college? And what for? To chase ghosts and shadows?

A plate of fritto misto sat between herself and Costanza's Uncle Mauro, one lightly battered piece of squid sitting alone on a white plate drizzled with olive oil and balsamic vinegar.

"Have it," she said.

"Are you sure?" Mauro asked, his smile beaming from ear to ear. "You are so generous."

"You're paying," Mia replied. "It's yours. Please, take it."

Mauro plucked the lonely squid ring from the plate and popped it into his mouth, dabbing his lips with a napkin as he devoured the expertly fried food. "Delicious," he said. "I wish we could get calamari like that back home."

Mia didn't answer. She still couldn't get the sight of Costanza disappearing among a sea of bodies out of her head.

"She'll come around," Mauro said, seemingly reading her mind. "She always does."

"I don't know," Mia replied. "This time she seemed serious."

Mauro chuckled. "The one thing you need to know about Italians is that we are an emotional species. One minute we're all laughter and song; the next, we're riled up and angry. Costanza will realize she's being a diva and come running back to you. You just need to give her time."

Mia peeked down at her phone again, willing it to ring.

"Back into focus," Mauro said, snapping his fingers. "We still have things to do."

"I don't know. I can't concentrate."

"Nonsense. I'm paying you, am I not?" he said, his hands dancing on the table. "Now listen, we have to figure out why."

Mia's eyes narrowed. "What do you mean?"

"Imperiis, Mia, remember? He's in that casket. His monogram proves it, but why? Why him and not Carmagnola?"

Mia let out a long sigh. "It's been a long day," she said. "We're both exhausted and sleep-deprived. Maybe we should call it a day and reset. We'll both think much more clearly after a good night's sleep."

"No, Mia. Now!" Mauro cried, slapping the table and causing her to jolt. "I need your brain. We are so close. So, so close. I have never felt so positive about this before. I just know we are going to get there, but it has to be now, while we're both in the moment."

Mia eyed her phone once more. If only Costanza would call, if only she would come back to her, but was that evenly remotely possible? She had been so angry, so disappointed in her. Why should she waste her time thinking about their relationship when Costanza had just disregarded her feelings like that? Maybe she should do what Mauro had asked and focus on solving the mystery. It would help take her mind off her failing love life, after all.

"Okay," she said, pushing the cell phone away. "Let's consider this. Imperiis was secretary of the council at the time Carmagnola was executed, so in that respect, the timeline matches, although we have to consider it doesn't line up with the murder of Alvise Della Torre, so that part of the story doesn't really work at all."

"Precisely," Mauro said, nodding energetically. "I like how you're thinking, Mia. You're on the right lines. I know it."

"We know the doge ordered Carmagnola's execution, and we also know that he wouldn't have done so without having the backing of the council."

"No, the doge wouldn't have taken such a drastic step without support."

"So we have to assume the council were behind it," Mia replied. "If the remains in that casket are really those of the secretary, then it's possible somebody had him killed without authorization and used the casket to hide the evidence."

"I like that!" Mauro cried, causing the couple on the table next to them to look up from their meals.

"And why would somebody go to the great trouble of having the secretary of the Council of Ten murdered?" Mia asked, now completely engrossed in theorizing.

"Because he did something to upset them," Mauro asked.

"And what better way of upsetting somebody than orchestrating the murder of a military commander?"

"Carmagnola!" Mauro replied. "You think Imperiis was the one pulling the strings."

"I don't know," Mia said. "But I believe it's highly probable."

"But who would do such a thing?" Mauro asked. "The secretary was an esteemed member of the palace. Killing him would be a risky move."

"Which means only someone with a clear motive would do so," Mia replied. "And what better motive than the murder of your husband?"

"Carmagnola's wife, Antonia," Mauro replied. "I think you're right. That would make perfect sense."

"She had the secretary killed," Mia said, now lost in her thoughts. "And then she used her links with the Catholic Church to hide the body in plain sight."

"It's so perfect," Mauro said. "Why didn't I think of that?"

"The only question is, what does Alvise Della Torre have to do with it? Why, when they opened the casket, was it his remains they found?"

"The friars," Mauro said. "They had to be in on it."

"It makes sense," Mia replied, slowly piecing everything together. "You said the Prior of the Basilica at that time was the Confessor of the Carmagnola family, so it's possible Carmagnola's wife convinced him to help keep Imperiis's murder a secret for centuries after."

"Using the remains of another murdered nobleman as a red herring to distract anybody interested enough to go poking their noses into their affairs."

"And take Imperiis's remains out and swap them with Della Torre's until the investigation was over."

"So where are Della Torre's remains now?" Mauro asked.

"Somewhere beneath the basilica, I would bet," Mia replied.

"Perhaps in the courtyard."

Mauro reached into his wallet and threw a wad of notes onto the table. "Then that's where we'll go," he said, grabbing his jacket.

"What? Now?" Mia exclaimed.

"I have to know," he replied, heading for the door. "I just have to."

Venice, Italy – 1432

Antonia drifted along the dark alleyway, her eyes downcast, hood pulled over her head. A rat ran across the bridge to her right, but she paid it no attention. She was still riven with grief and rage. Somebody had to pay for her husband's brutal murder. Two men appeared from between two buildings, one of them so drunk he could barely stand, and the other attempting to hold him up. She moved around them like a phantom, keeping to the shadows so as not to allow herself to be recognized. What she was planning required complete discretion. Nobody could know what was going to happen.

Further along the street, she approached a doorway. It was old, weather-beaten, like the hull of an aging ship. She rapped on it twice, and after a few moments, an old man appeared, his face like old leather, eyes darting within sunken sockets. He looked her up and down, and for a moment she thought she had the wrong house, but then his face broke into a broad grin, his rotting teeth protruding from barren gums like gray stones. He wore a half-dozen rings of fine gems on his withered fingers, but his knuckles were cracked and bruised.

"Signora," he said, his voice like broken glass. "You're early."

"Only a little," she replied. "I wanted to make sure you'd be here."

"I never let a client down," the man said, feigning offense. "Not one as pretty as you."

"Have you received my instructions and your compensation?" she asked, cutting to the chase.

"Of course. It's an honor to be of service to you."

"I want it done as soon as possible," she replied, handing over a small bag of gleaming coins.

"Tonight it is, then," he replied, slipping the bag into his pocket. "And given your generosity, I propose an additional service, on the house, of course."

Antonia raised an eyebrow.

"It's a matter of the occult," he whispered. "I'm well aware that you despise the man you have asked me to take care of, and with such a level of pure hatred, quite often, only a curse will do."

"A curse?"

"The gift has been in my family for generations," he said. "The curse of the damned. When the man in question is dead, I will cast a hex over his body, meaning that his family will never know peace, and his loved ones will be forever chased by a dark cloud of misfortune and torment."

As Antonia considered his words, the old man beckoned a stranger from the shadows: a tall man wrapped in a dark cloak with eyes as cold as the deepest parts of the ocean. Within an instant, he handed the gentleman the coins, which slipped beneath the cloak and out of sight.

"A location," the sicario said, head tilted to the side to keep the light of the moon from revealing his features. "We need to know where to dispose of the body."

Antonia smiled, but it was a grim sneer of satisfaction, not joy. "Don't worry. I have a place in mind."

A loud knock sounded on the door of the Basilica of Santa Maria Gloriosa dei Frari at around midnight, causing Fra Dolphi to race across the nave. As the door opened a crack, his heart sank. Three men stood outside with a black casket hidden between them. The sicario at the head of the party gestured to the inside of the basilica, and the friar turned, hastening the other friars to bring the casket in from the street.

As the men hoisted the black box across the threshold, the three sicarios disappeared, the only evidence that they'd ever been there the soft patter of footsteps in the distance.

Fra Dolphi walked toward the doorway to the cloister on the right hand aisle of the church and urged his men to hitch the casket to the ropes hanging from the makeshift scaffold they had built around the exit. With the casket now high above the door, they fixed it to the stone structure with wooden brackets and metal fixings.

The friar stood there, arms folded, peering up at the newly located coffin, and allowed himself a wry smile of satisfaction.

"Where better to hide the secrets of the Carmagnola family than in plain sight?" he said before turning and disappearing into the darkness.

Venice, Italy – 1549

The Council of Ten sat in the great chamber of Palazzo Ducale and discussed the next item of business. One of the loyal members of Venetian nobility had been violently murdered by a rival family, and although justice was yet to be served, it was up to the council to decide where the deceased man would be interred.

"He needs a burial of some note," one of the councilmen said. "His family deserve as much."

"But we shouldn't allow it to become too extravagant," the treasurer said. "Our pockets are not as deep as they once were."

"Perhaps a good location rather than an expensive service," another added. "His family would like that."

"We must consider his lineage," a fourth member said. "These are good people, and what's more, they offer valuable donations to the cause."

"I was at the Basilica of Santa Maria Gloriosa dei Frari just the other day," one of them said. "Are you familiar with the infamous black casket?"

"The one that sits above the door to the cloister?" another asked. "Yes, I have seen it many times."

"Well, it is empty," the councilor replied. "It would be an impressive place to inter a fine man such as Della Torre."

"I like that idea," the lead councilor said. "It shows our generosity, but also our sense of duty to the Catholic Church."

"His family will be very pleased," another added. "It's a wonderful suggestion."

"Then summon the prior," the leader replied. "The quicker we get this done, the better for all those involved."

"The funeral is being held in his hometown," the prior said to his friars. "They'll bring his body here after proceedings, which means we have a chance to prepare before they arrive."

"Our Lord is looking over us," a young friar replied.

"Indeed," said the prior. "I have convinced them to allow us to inter the body at night, away from prying eyes." He looked toward the cloister. "Did you finish painting the Della Torre crest above the doorway?"

One of the friars at the back of the room nodded. "Just as you asked."

"Then it is done," the prior said.

"But where will we put the body, if not in the casket?" a tall friar with a narrow face asked.

The prior pointed to the courtyard. "You have shovels, don't you?"

The friars nodded their silent confirmation.

"Then get to work. There's a hole to be dug."

CHAPTER TWENTY-ONE

VENICE – PRESENT DAY

Costanza stood on the platform, looking at the train to Milan, thinking about her fiancée out there with her uncle, making the same mistakes over and over again. She loved her so much, but this obsession of hers was just crazy. She wished she'd never introduced her to her zio. She wished they'd turned down his suggestion of a holiday in Venice. The whole thing had been a disaster from start to finish.

Her phone rang in her hand, and thinking it was Mia, she answered it instantly.

"Have you come to your senses yet?" she asked.

"Costanza, it's me, your cousin," came the voice down the line.

"Ben?" she asked. "Is it really you?"

"It is," he said. "I've been trying to get hold of Dad, but he's not picking up."

Costanza pictured her uncle running around Piazza San Marco, chasing the ghost of a curse he could never find. "He's... busy at the moment," she replied. "In fact, he's been extremely busy ever since we got here."

"I'm worried about him," Ben said. "His heart. It can't take too much stress."

"I'm sure he's fine," Costanza replied, trying to hide her own anxiety. "He'll be home before you know it."

"Can you... can you just tell him I love him?" Ben said. "If you see him, I mean. I just have this awful feeling that something bad's going to happen."

"Of course I'll tell him," Costanza replied, eyeing her carryon case and the train that lay waiting like a sleeping tiger. "I'll tell him right away, but honestly, Ben. You don't need to worry. Your father's as strong as a bull, with the energy of a man half his age."

"Thank you, Costanza," Ben said. "You've always had a way of making me feel better."

Costanza felt a pang of guilt as she ended the call and turned toward the exit. Maybe she wasn't leaving Venice so soon after all.

Mauro and Mia sneaked back into the basilica, taking care not to draw attention to themselves. Once inside, they once more maneuvered the cherry picker to a spot beneath the casket.

"I'm going up," Mauro said, stumbling toward it, breathing heavily.

"No, I'll go," Mia replied. "You don't look too well."

"I'm fine," Mauro said. "Just a little full from dinner. I can do it."

"No you can't," Mia interjected. "And anyway, you've been up there already. I want to take a look for myself."

"You know, Costanza's right about you," Mauro said. "You can be quite stubborn."

"And you can be a pain," Mia shot back. "Now stand back while I raise the platform."

Mauro conceded the argument. "Okay, but remember the plan. We need a few hairs so that we can get a good sample for DNA testing. It's the only way we'll know for sure."

"I know how DNA testing works," Mia replied.

As she steered the cherry picker to the level of the casket, Costanza appeared from the gloom, a look of shock on her face.

"Zio!" she exclaimed. "Mia!"

"You scared the living daylights out of me!" Mauro cried. "What are you doing here? I thought you wanted no part of this."

"It's great to see you," Mia said, looking down at her fiancée, wishing she could take her in her arms and tell her everything was going to be okay.

"I took a call from Ben," Costanza said. "He's worried about you, Zio. He told me to tell you how much he loves you."

Mauro's expression shifted, but only a little. "We're almost done," he replied.

"No, you are done," Costanza said. "Don't you see? We need to leave Venice straight away. You look worse than ever, and this place? It's not good for you."

"I can't leave, Costanza. I can't. I need to break it."

"Break what?" Costanza asked. "The casket? This heavy load that's been hanging around your neck?"

"No! The curse!" he hollered, sweat pouring from his face. "I have to break the curse!"

Mia climbed down from the cherry picker, just as a dark figure emerged from the shadows.

"Nobody move," Wallace said, a grave smirk on his lips.

"You brought him here!" Mauro said, pointing accusingly at Costanza.

"No, I didn't know he was following me."

"I'm trying to save our family, but you have betrayed us!" Mauro cried.

"If you cooperate, I'll do what I can to ensure you get favorable treatment," Wallace said.

Mauro shot Mia a despairing look before running to the exit, Wallace in hot pursuit.

"I told you," Costanza said to Mia. "I told you this wouldn't end well."

"Cos, I—" Mia said, but Costanza was already chasing after her uncle. She followed behind, running as fast as she could but realizing they were in way over their heads. Things were happening that they couldn't control, and they were being swept up in a tide that threatened to wash them all out into the vastness of the ocean.

Mauro's heart was pounding in his chest so hard he could barely see straight. How could she do this to him? His own niece. His own flesh and blood. She'd brought the inspector to his door, knowing that his arrival would halt his ambitions. He'd had the curse in his sights and the secrets of the black casket within his grasp. Now all of that was for nothing. The inspector knew. He knew everything. If he ever allowed him to catch up with him, the truth would come out. His family would never speak to him again. He would be alone once more with only his grandfather's notebook to keep him company.

He raced to the Piazza San Marco because it was the one place he knew well, the place where the Count of Carmagnola had died and this whole sorry business began. He could see the columns in the distance, the water beyond. If only he could go back in time and ensure things had been done differently. If only his ancestor hadn't convinced the Council of Ten to go along with his devious plan. Perhaps his father would still be alive, or would at least have ended his life in peace.

He could hear Wallace behind him, his heavy feet pouncing on the stone beneath them. The guy was overweight but he was fitter than he looked. Mauro's heart, however, was weak, and he could feel it straining at the leash, almost at bursting point. He could barely breathe, could barely run in a straight line, but he couldn't be caught. He wouldn't allow himself to be snared.

The columns were close now, the place where Carmagnola was beheaded. He could almost see the crowds surrounding the executioner's platform and hear Antonia's screams as the blade came down, again and again. He had to stop. He couldn't go on any longer. He had no strength, no oxygen. His heart was smashing into his breastbone repeatedly, kicking like an old horse. He looked up at the Lion and San Teodoro, the two heavenly figures bearing witness to his final judgement, and he fell to his knees, his lungs now starved of air. As Wallace called out his name, and a young couple raced to his aid, he pitched forward, and his head came to rest at the exact spot where the bloodstains of an unjustified execution could never truly be washed away.

CHAPTER TWENTY-TWO

VENICE – LAKE 1800S

The friar walked across the courtyard, his hands folded in front of him. He had news for the prior, and it wasn't good. They had been so dutiful, so diligent in keeping with the oath their ancestors had made, but now their fortitude was being tested. He didn't know how to break the news. He just knew he couldn't hide it any longer.

"I have received word," he said to the prior. "The rumors proved to be true. The government wants to inspect the contents of the casket."

The prior shook his head. "After all these years, now they want to know."

"It is the sway of public opinion," the friar replied. "The people of Venice have become more and more curious. It is this curiosity that has convinced the government officials to prove once and for all that Alvise Della Torre is the man whose remains rest above that doorway."

"But we know they do not," the prior said. "Which gives us a very serious problem indeed."

Over the following two days, the friars did something they never thought they would have to do, and when the work was done, they delivered the casket to the very people tasked with conducting an investigation, and prayed to God that the answer that came back would be the right one.

The prior sat in his room, sipping warm tea and waiting for his friar to return. If everything went the way they had planned, they still had a lot of work to do, but if it didn't, the whole of Italy would turn to them requesting answers. He couldn't even begin to plan what to do in that eventuality, because it was as unprecedented as the sun refusing to rise in the morning.

When the door opened, his breath caught in his throat. This was it.

"I have the results," the friar said, holding a slip of parchment between his narrow fingers.

"Well then tell me, man," the prior replied. "Don't keep me waiting. I barely slept last night."

"The result was conclusive," the friar said. "The clothes proved it was Della Torre."

"Praise God!" the prior exclaimed. "Swapping the remains worked."

"It appears so," the friar replied.

The prior stood and approached his friend, taking his hand in his. "This is good work," he said. "But we have more to do. Tonight, when the basilica is closed, we switch the remains back."

"But why?" the friar asked, looking confused. "Imperiis died hundreds of years ago. What does it matter if he remains in the ground and Della Torre remains in the casket? Isn't it easier if we just leave them where they are?"

"Easier doesn't come into it," the prior said. "We made an oath to someone who did much for this basilica, and I will not be the prior to break that sacred promise."

"But it doesn't make any sense," the friar said.

"It depends on your point of view," the prior replied. "But as men of honor, we obey the bidding of those that came before us. To do anything else would be wholly inappropriate. Tonight we dig, and by sunrise, Imperiis will be back where he belongs."

That night, the friars worked diligently, digging up the remains they'd kept hidden from the government officials, while carefully removing Della Torre from the casket and lowering his ashes into the ground. When Imperiis was once more laid in his final resting place, the lid was sealed, and the friars bowed their heads, saying one last prayer as the first glow of the new day began to peek through the stained-glass windows. The great deception was complete, and the memory of the Count of Carmagnola had been honored. His wife would have been pleased. Very pleased.

CHAPTER TWENTY-THREE

VENICE – PRESENT DAY

Federica Genovese stood outside the hospital room, her head in her hands. If she had known her brother would have gone so crazy about the contents of that damn casket, she would never have suggested her daughter and her fiancée go with him. Instead, she would have accompanied her brother and made sure he didn't do something stupid. She took a deep breath, waited for her racing heart to steady a little, and opened the door.

"Federica, my love," Mauro said, his voice weak and cracked. "Come in, come in. It's such a pleasure to see you."

"You are a damn fool, brother," Federica said. "Your heart is too weak for this kind of excitement."

"Excitement doesn't even begin to describe it," Mauro replied, his complexion sallow, his skin the color of ash.

"If I had known—" Federica said, her voice breaking. "Mauro, I'm so sorry."

"Sorry for what, sister? For letting me spend some time with my niece?"

"For allowing you to go off on such a foolish, harmful errand."

"There was no harm in what we did, Federica. Quite the opposite. We came close. So, so close."

Federica took her brother's hand in hers and felt the icy touch of his fragile skin. It was like taking the old bones of a corpse, only this corpse had eyes, lips, a voice.

"Did you bring it?" he asked.

"Did I bring what?"

"The journal. Did Mia give it to you?"

Federica nodded. "Of course she did, but what does it matter now?"

"Of course it matters," he said, pausing as a bout of coughing took hold of him, and before long, he was heaving and retching into a handkerchief. "Everything matters. Nothing has changed."

"Look at you!" Federica exclaimed. "Everything has changed. You're barely able to hold a conversation, Mauro. You should never have put yourself through this. The doctor, he says you almost died out there in the piazza."

"And if the inspector had his way, perhaps I might have," Mauro replied. "That man has been pursuing me from the start."

"Costanza told me what you said about her," Federica hissed. "How could you accuse her like that?"

"I wasn't thinking straight," Mauro replied. "But now I see clearly. I see everything in brilliant technicolor. Wallace was the enemy all along. Not Costanza, not Mia. If we can just steer clear of him, we can get to the bottom of—"

"Will you stop?" Federica asked. "Will you just stop for one goddamn minute? The enemy isn't the inspector, or my daughter, or her fiancée."

"Who, then?"

"Don't you see? It's you, Mauro. You're your own worst enemy. You would never have had this heart attack, and perhaps Susan would never have disappeared, if you had just left well enough alone. The mystery of the casket died with our father, and you should have let it lay in peace in the grave we dug for him."

"But that's not true," Mauro said, attempting to sit up. "The curse still exists. The casket still holds the secrets. If we don't chase this through to its rightful conclusion, then Ben, Costanza, and all the other family members who come after them will be cursed, just as we have been cursed, and our parents and grandparents before us."

"That's just a fallacy," Federica said. "An old myth dreamed up by people who should have known better."

Mauro eyed her bag. "Is it in there?" he asked. "The journal, I mean."

Federica clutched her handbag to her chest. "It is, but it will stay with me. Nobody can be allowed to follow this crazy path you've been treading. It only leads to upset."

"You must give it to Ben," he said, reaching for her with grasping, clawing hands. "Please, Federica, you have to give it to him. It's a matter of life and death."

"No it's not, Mauro. It's just a book. A stupid book."

"It's not stupid!" he yelled. "You always say such negative things. You have to believe me. You have to... believe in... the curse."

He slumped back on his pillow, too out of breath to continue.

"Oh, Mauro," Federica said. "Look at you. Just look at you. This compulsion of yours, it will be the death of you. It has made you so ill, I can barely even stand it."

"He has... to have the journal. Please... Federica... you have to give it... to him. I know now... the corpse... the murder... the friars hid it high up there in plain view. Nobody would ever suspect… "

"I will," she said, tears welling in her eyes. "Despite what I believe, if it makes you happy, I'll make sure he gets it."

"And tell him... no matter who gets in... his way... no matter the financial cost... no matter... what obstacles present themself... to him, he has to... pursue this to the end. He... has to... rid our family of... the curse."

Federica took his hand in hers as a tear slipped down her cheek. She wanted to tell him this was all just a crazy notion and that to pass the journal on to his son would be like passing on a sickness, but she also knew that her brother wasn't strong enough to hear those words. She clung onto him like the captain of a rescue vessel clinging to the survivor of a sinking ship, hoping and praying she could haul him aboard and save his life. She loved her brother, even if he could be the most frustrating, annoying individual she'd ever met. He was her blood, the older brother she'd followed around when she was young, looking up to him in a way that only younger siblings could.

"I... have one last... favor," he asked, his fingers hanging from her like old vines. "Will you do... it for me?"

"Of course," Federica said, dabbing her eyes with a handkerchief. "Anything. Whatever you want."

"Will you... make sure my... Susan receives a proper... burial?"

"What?" Federica exclaimed, believing she'd misheard him.

"I must have... aggravated the curse... by refusing her a proper... interment," he said. "You need... to ensure... she gets one."

"I don't understand," Federica replied. "Susan is missing. How can I bury someone who's not dead?"

"I didn't... mean it," he whispered.

"Mean what?" Federica asked, shocked at how dark her brother's eyes had become. His body seemed to be sinking into the bed, as if the Earth was taking back something it owned. "Mauro, what didn't you mean?"

"I swear," he said, his voice little more than a coarse hiss. "I swear I didn't... mean to do... what I did."

As Federica stooped to hear her brother's words, he drew in a gasping breath, and then there was rattle from his throat like something breaking, and he went still, his chest no longer moving, and his eyes like tiny black balls that no longer perceived a life that had somehow drifted away.

"Mauro," she said. "Mauro, are you okay?" She turned to the door. "Nurse!" she hollered. "Nurse, my brother needs help. He needs... he needs..."

As the door opened and the medical staff came charging in, Federica sobbed into her hands, her shoulder shuddering as everything came crashing in on her. He was gone, Mauro was gone, and there was nothing any of them could do about it.

Mia stood outside by the fountain while Costanza paced anxiously. They'd been waiting for what seemed like hours. Their trip to Venice hadn't panned out the way they'd hoped. It had stretched their relationship to breaking point, and had made Costanza's uncle so terribly ill.

When Federica appeared, it was like a welcome relief, but the look on her face told Mia something was wrong.

"How did it go?" Costanza asked, taking her mother in her arms.

"Was he awake?" Mia asked.

"I spoke to him," Federica said, nodding as best she could, but then the tears came.

"Mom, what's wrong?" Costanza asked.

"He's gone," Federica replied through her sobs. "Oh, Costanza! Your uncle's gone!"

The three of them hugged, the finality of the situation almost too much to bear.

After a moment, Federica reached into her bag with trembling hands, grabbed the journal, and tossed it into the water.

"That's the last this family will see of that damn thing!" she said. "It's brought nothing but bad luck to all of us."

Mia watched the journal as it slowly slipped beneath the surface, and she wondered how the story really ended.

"I need a moment," Federica said, dabbing at her eyes as she headed back inside.

"I don't know what to say," Costanza said, the shock evident in her eyes.

"I can't believe he's gone," Mia replied, remembering the man who'd taught her so much about the mysteries of Venice.

"I'll miss him," Costanza said.

"Me too," Mia said. "But not as much as I've missed you." She took Costanza's hand, and to her surprise, her fiancée let her do it.

"We have some making up to do," Costanza replied, smiling.

As they walked along the water's edge, the bells of the basilica rang out, and across Venice, thousands of happy travelers listened with open ears and willing hearts.

EPILOGUE: HOUSTON - FIVE YEARS LATER

Ben stood in the front room of the house he'd shared with his parents many years ago and watched as the removal men walked backward and forward, carrying furniture, the large screen TV, and the antique coffee table his mom had bought in an auction. Outside, the realtor stood with a clipboard in his hands, checking everything as it was loaded into the waiting truck.

"You know, I think you're really going to miss this place," he said to Ben. "You grew up here, didn't you?"

"Yep," Ben replied. "But I'm married now, and it's time for my wife and me to get a place of our own."

"At least you sold at the peak," the realtor replied. "Your mom and dad would be really pleased."

"Maybe," Ben said. "Although I think they'd hoped I'd stay here forever, you know?"

The realtor turned and looked at the roman helmet one of the removal men was holding. "We'll itemize all this stuff before it's put up for auction," he said. "Let you know what we've got and how much we're likely to make."

"Kind of makes me sad," Ben said. "My mom spent most of her life pulling this collection together, but ever since she disappeared and my father passed, it just gives me bad vibes."

"I know exactly what you mean," the realtor said. "My parents left me a first edition copy of Moby Dick, but ever since they died in a boating accident, it's stayed in the basement beneath a ton of boxes. I couldn't even begin to think about looking at it. Did they ever... find out what happened to your mother?"

Ben shook his head. "No. The inspector on the case retired, and since then, there's been nothing. Maybe she ran off, maybe somebody took her. I guess I'll never really know."

"Must be hard," the realtor said. "I mean, at least I know what happened to my parents. You must want closure."

"Closure would be good," Ben replied. "But I'm afraid the investigation's now been labeled a cold case. That means no resources, no reports, and no investigations. The only way I'd find my mom is if she came looking for me, and I'm afraid that's pretty unlikely."

"You never know," the realtor replied. "Stranger things have happened."

"Well, I'll take the bet if you're willing to put money on it," Ben said. "Listen, I've got a ton of stuff to go through, so—"

"Not at all," the realtor replied, pressing the beeper to his Mercedes. "I'll head back into the office and send you an email once all this is done and dusted."

"Sure thing," Ben said and headed to the pile of ancient artifacts the removers had piled up in the entranceway. He ran a hand over a shield that had once adorned the fireplace, and a spear that had stood in the corner of the dining room like a silent sentry. These were things he would miss, but they were also things he would be glad to never see again. He wanted no part of the life that had decimated his family, nor the obsession that had torn them apart.

As he stood there, ruminating over a life that had shifted beneath him many years prior, a loud crash came from the direction of the hallway. He ran toward it, fearing that one of the workers had fallen and injured themselves, but when he got there, two of the removal men stood sheepishly by a tall Roman urn that had once been used in ancient times to bury children. He remembered clearly that it had always been hanging high up there in the two story entryway. The lid of the urn now lay on the floor with a huge crack down the center.

"I'm sorry, sir," one of them said. "We were lifting it, and it just slipped."

Ben eyed the broken lid and thought about that. What did it matter? This stuff was all being sold anyway, and there was so much of it. One little lid wasn't going to put a dent in the top line.

"It's okay," he said. "Don't worry about it."

The men looked confused. "It's not... the lid we're worried about, sir. It's... what we found."

Ben shook his head. "What are you talking about?"

"The urn," one of the men said, eyeing the open container. "There's something... inside it. Something... bad."

Ben approached the artifact, its open mouth like an angry wound. He crossed the hallway, wondering what could be inside an urn he'd walked past thousands of times since his mother had bought it, but when he got close, his mouth fell open and a scream built in his lungs. He couldn't believe it. It was like something out of a hellish nightmare.

The body inside was bent over double like a baby in the womb, except this was no baby, and the urn was no womb. It was the woman who had carried him for nine months and raised him, teaching him how to read, how to play the piano, and how to ride a bicycle. He hadn't seen her for over eight years, but he recognized her in an instant because she was wearing the same blue dress he had last seen her in on the night she never came home. She hadn't vanished. She'd been right under their noses all along, buried in plain sight.

"Mom!" he cried. "Oh, God! Mom!"

It was a sunny day in Venice. The air was warm, the water as still as glass. A group of kids ran up and down the waterway, tossing stones and laughing and joking. It was the kind of day made for energetic children, and these kids were going to enjoy it until their parents hollered for them to come inside.

A young boy, Enzo, stood at the water's edge, his net cast into the canal, hoping and praying he might catch a fish. He'd been trying all day, but there had been nothing. He still had time, though. One more hour and who knows? He might just catch the biggest fish of all.

"Come on, Enzo," a girl, Giulia, cried. "You've been messing around with that thing for ages. Let's see what you've caught."

"I think I just have trash in there," Enzo said.

"Well, then, let's see."

Enzo liked Giulia almost as much as he liked fish, so he relented, hauling the net out of the water and tipping its contents onto the ground.

"Cool!" Giulia cried. "There's lots of things."

She was right. There was an old tin can, a sparkling pair of sunglasses, a disposable vape, and something else. A book, maybe.

"Let's have a look at that," Giulia said, reaching for the leather-bound journal.

"No, it's mine," Enzo replied, stooping down and collecting it in his hands.

"Is that a treasure map?" Enzo's friend, Rocco asked.

Enzo had no idea, but he secretly hoped so. As he began to turn the pages, old notes appeared, followed by sketches, and handwriting in a thick scrawl. It was the strangest notebook he'd ever seen.

"Oh, it's just some old tourist crap," Rocco said. "Toss it back in the canal."

As Rocco and Giulia lost interest and headed back to their bicycles, Enzo kept looking. The words and pictures fascinated him. It was like a story about a world he didn't understand, and the thought excited him. Once he'd had a chance to study the journal in more detail, he'd know everything about this strange book and the people who had written it. He just needed to be patient.

He would hide it where nobody would find it. He would be the only one who would know about it, and one day, when he had the money and the ability to research what it said, he would follow it to its final chapter, and maybe what lay in wait at the end of the story was a truth so magical, it would make him rich beyond his wildest dreams.

www.ingramcontent.com/pod-product-compliance
Lightning Source LLC
Chambersburg PA
CBHW070553310726
48982CB00011B/1569/J

9798218891190